My Weird School graphic Novel

Ella MeNTRY School
"learn...or else"

Get a Grip! We're on a Trip!

New York Times Bestselling Author
Dan Gutman

Pictures by
Jim Paillot

HARPER alley

An Imprint of HarperCollinsPublishers

HarperAlley is an imprint of HarperCollins Publishers.

My Weird School Graphic Novel: Get a Grip! We're on a Trip!

Text copyright © 2022 by Dan Gutman

Illustrations copyright © 2022 by Jim Paillot

All rights reserved. Printed in Spain.

www.harpercollinschildrens.com

ISBN 978-0-06-305448-6 (pbk. bdg.) — ISBN 978-0-06-305452-3 (hardcover bdg.)

Typography by Martha Maynard

21 22 23 24 25   EP   10 9 8 7 6 5 4 3 2 1

❖

First Edition

Warning!

THIS BOOK CONTAINS SCENES OF GRAPHIC VIOLINS, AS WELL AS OTHER MUSICAL INSTRUMENTS. ALL CHARACTERS IN THIS BOOK ARE FICTIONAL. ANY RESEMBLANCE TO ACTUAL PERSONS, LIVING OR DEAD, IS ENTIRELY INTENTIONAL. ENTER AT YOUR OWN RISK. NO LIFEGUARD ON DUTY. HA-HA! HE SAID DUTY. YOU'RE ALLOWED TO SAY DUTY, BUT YOU'RE NOT SUPPOSED TO SAY DOODY. NOBODY KNOWS WHY. THEY SHOULD DEFINITELY HAVE NEW WORDS FOR DUTY AND DOODY THAT DON'T SOUND SO MUCH ALIKE.

OH, IT DOESN'T MATTER. YOU'RE PROBABLY NOT EVEN READING THIS ANYWAY. WHO WANTS TO READ A BUNCH OF WORDS SCRUNCHED TOGETHER THAT ARE ALL CAPITAL LETTERS? WORDS ARE FOR NERDS. BRING ON THE PICTURES.

Table of Contents*

*I'M **CONTENT** TO SIT ON A **TABLE**.

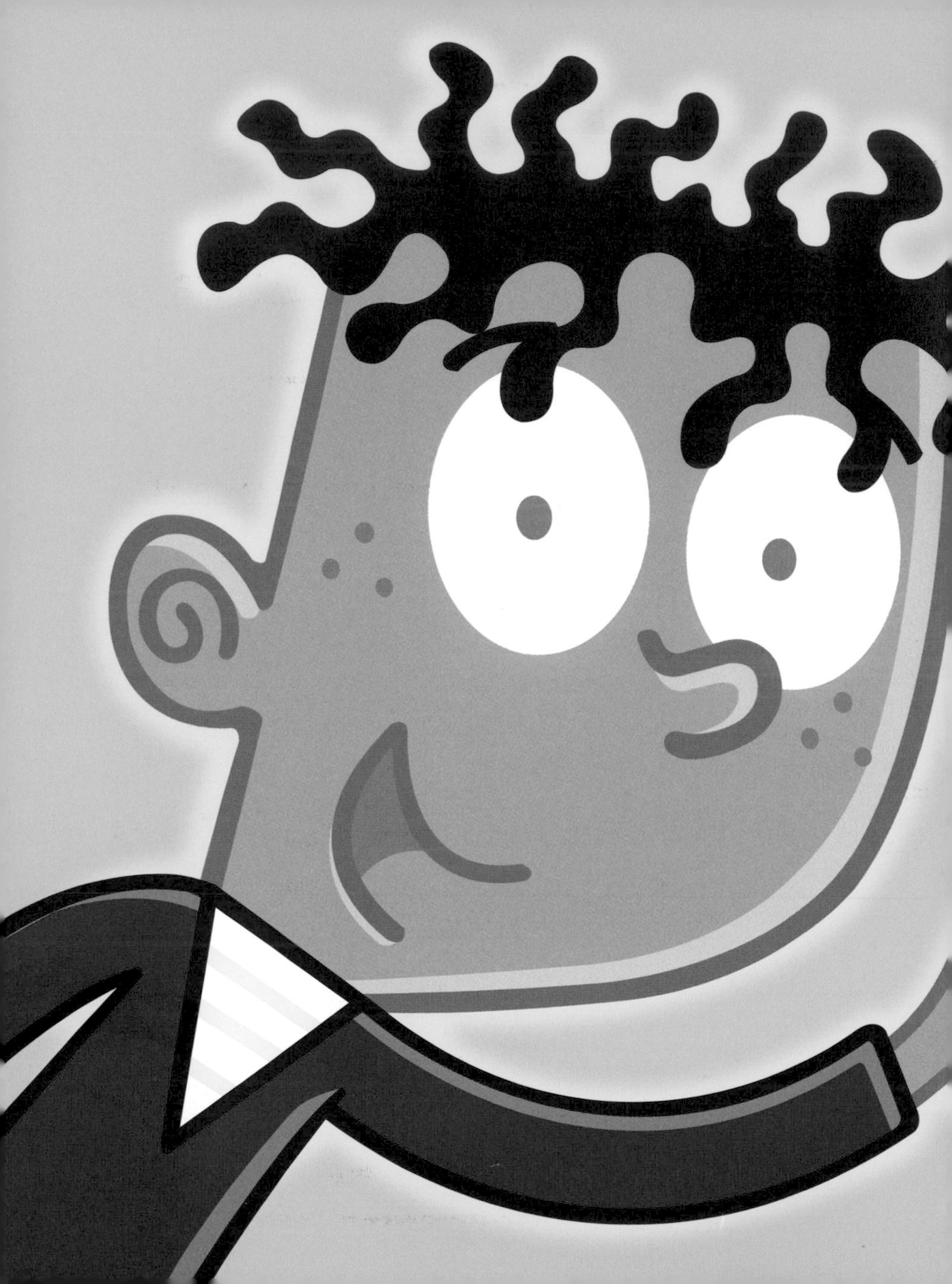

CHAPTER 1

Stuff

IT'S
RIDORKULOUS!

A short time ago in a school system not far away . . .

Episode I
The Big Jerk

IT IS A DARK TIME. SINISTER FORCES HAVE CAUSED UNREST IN THE UNIVERSE. UNDER THE LEADERSHIP OF THE EVIL AND EXTREMELY ANNOYING DR. CARBLES—THE PRESIDENT OF THE BOARD OF EDUCATION—TURMOIL* HAS ENGULFED* ELLA MENTRY SCHOOL. CARBLES AND HIS MERCILESS LEGIONS HAVE TRAVELED A MILLION HUNDRED LIGHT-YEARS TO ONCE AND FOR ALL CONFRONT MR. KLUTZ, HIS LONG-TIME ADVERSARY* AND BENEVOLENT PRINCIPAL. KLUTZ AND THE BRAVE RESISTANCE TEACHERS HAVE STRUGGLED TO MAINTAIN PEACE AND ORDER IN THE SCHOOL. BUT EVIL IS EVERYWHERE, AND TOILETS HAVE OVERFLOWED. MR. KLUTZ HAS MOUNTED A DESPERATE MISSION TO RESCUE THE BESIEGED SCHOOL, SAVE THE STUDENTS AND TEACHERS, AND RESTORE PEACE AND EDUCATION TO THE THIRD GRADE. LITTLE DOES HE KNOW THAT THE DIABOLICAL DR. CARBLES HAS DEVISED A PLAN THAT WILL SPELL CERTAIN DOOM FOR THE SMALL BAND OF TEACHERS AND STAFF STRUGGLING TO STAND AGAINST TYRANNY* AND RESTORE READING, WRITING, AND ARITHMETIC TO THE SCHOOL SYSTEM. IN AN ALARMING CHAIN OF EVENTS, DR. CARBLES HAS DEVISED A SECRET WEAPON THAT WILL HAVE THE CAPABILITY TO DESTROY AN ENTIRE ELEMENTARY SCHOOL. HE IS RUTHLESS AND DETERMINED TO VANQUISH ANY THREAT TO HIS POWER. HE WILL NOT REST UNTIL MR. KLUTZ AND ELLA MENTRY SCHOOL ARE NO MORE.

(*Oooh, big words! You must be a real smarty-pants.)

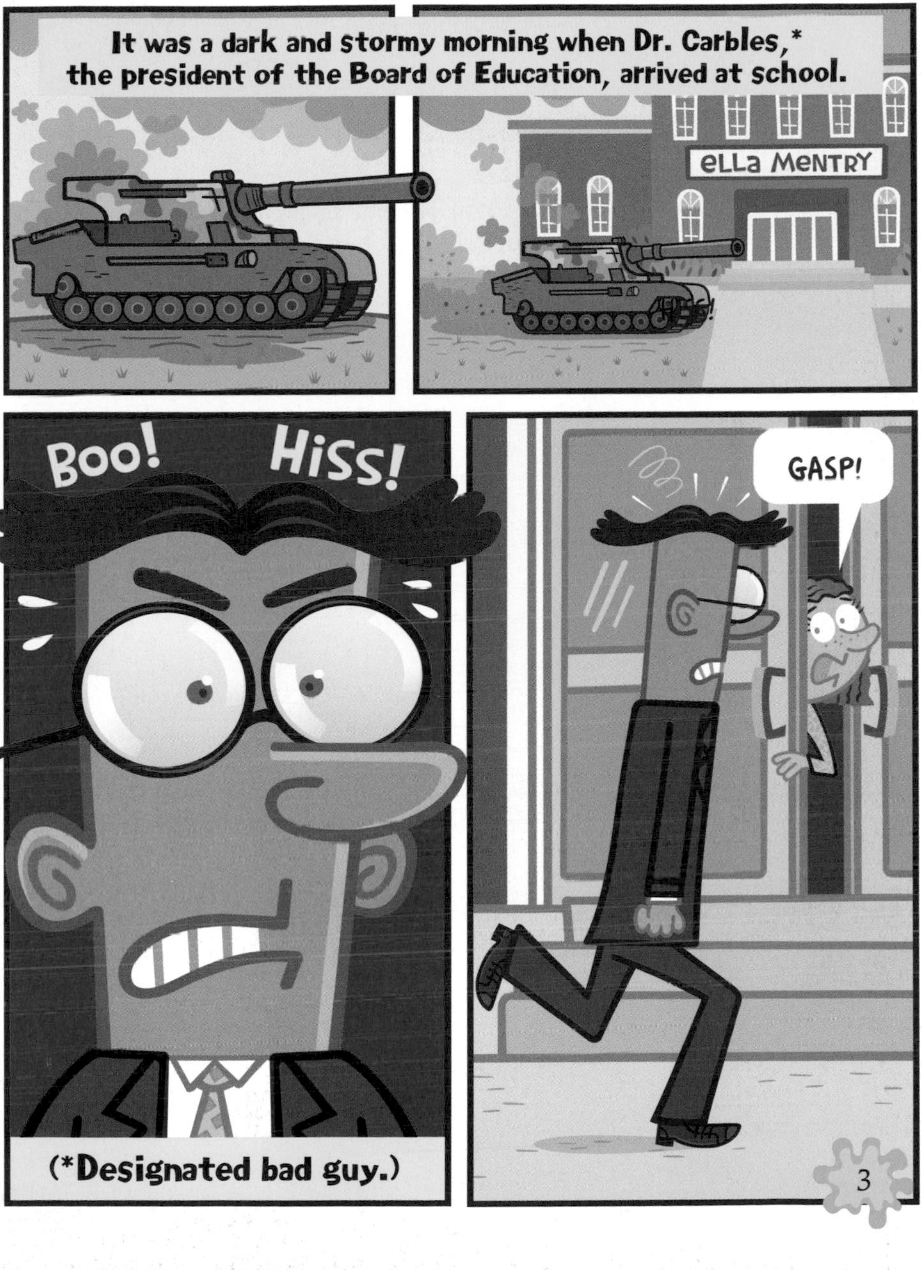
It was a dark and stormy morning when Dr. Carbles,* the president of the Board of Education, arrived at school.
ELLA MENTRY
BOO!
HISS!
(*Designated bad guy.)
GASP!

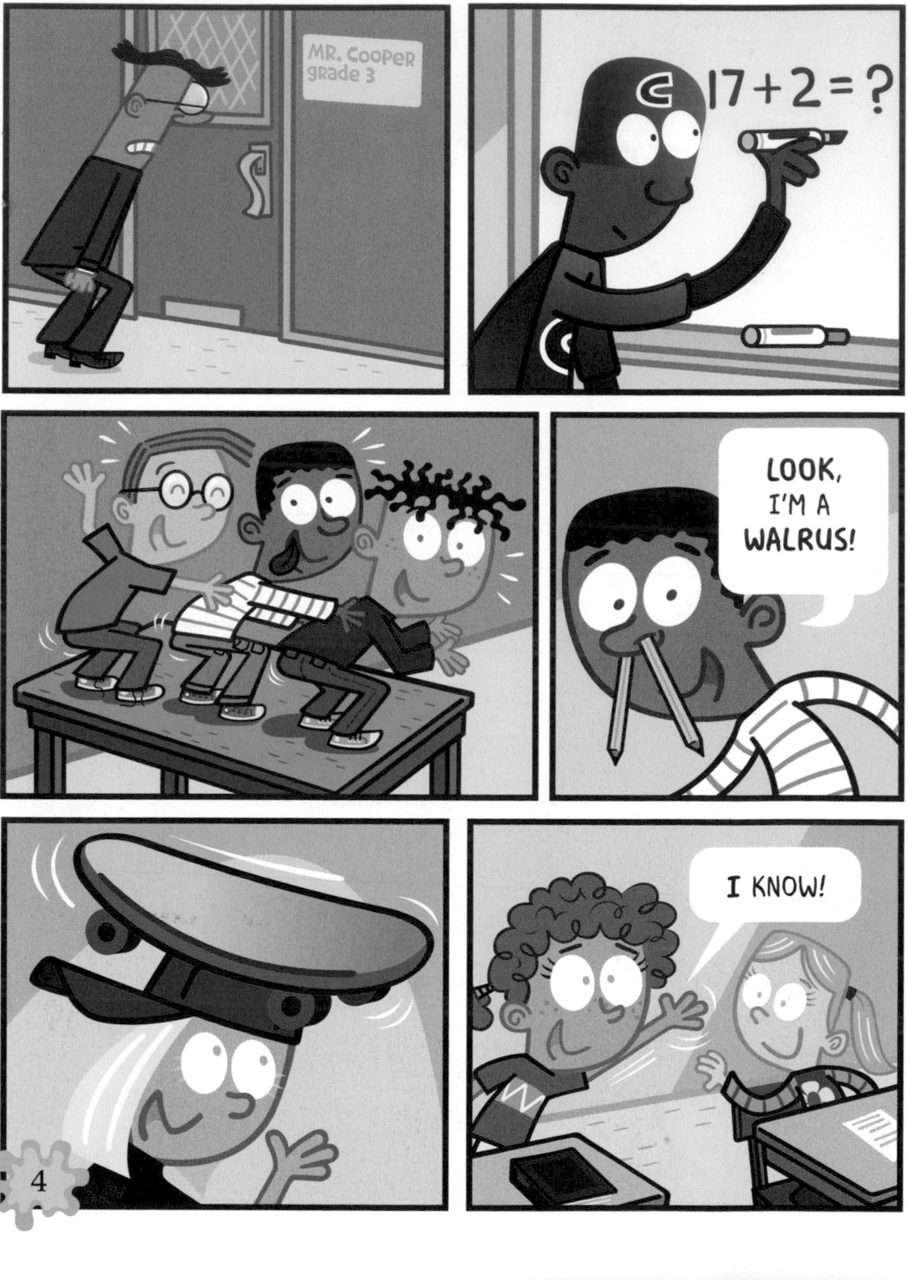
MR. COOPER
grade 3
17 + 2 = ?
LOOK, I'M A WALRUS!
I KNOW!

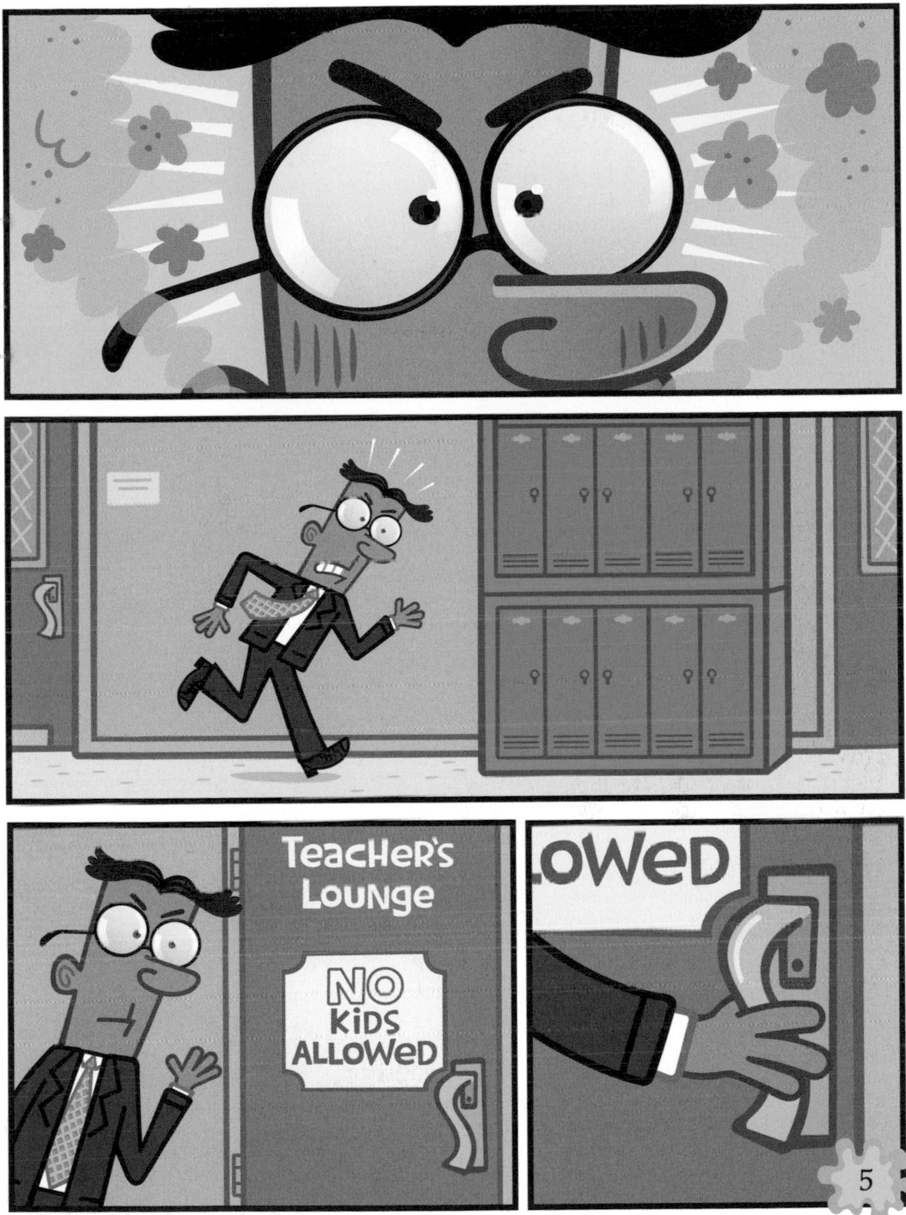
TEACHER'S
LOUNGE
NO
KIDS
ALLOWED
LOWED

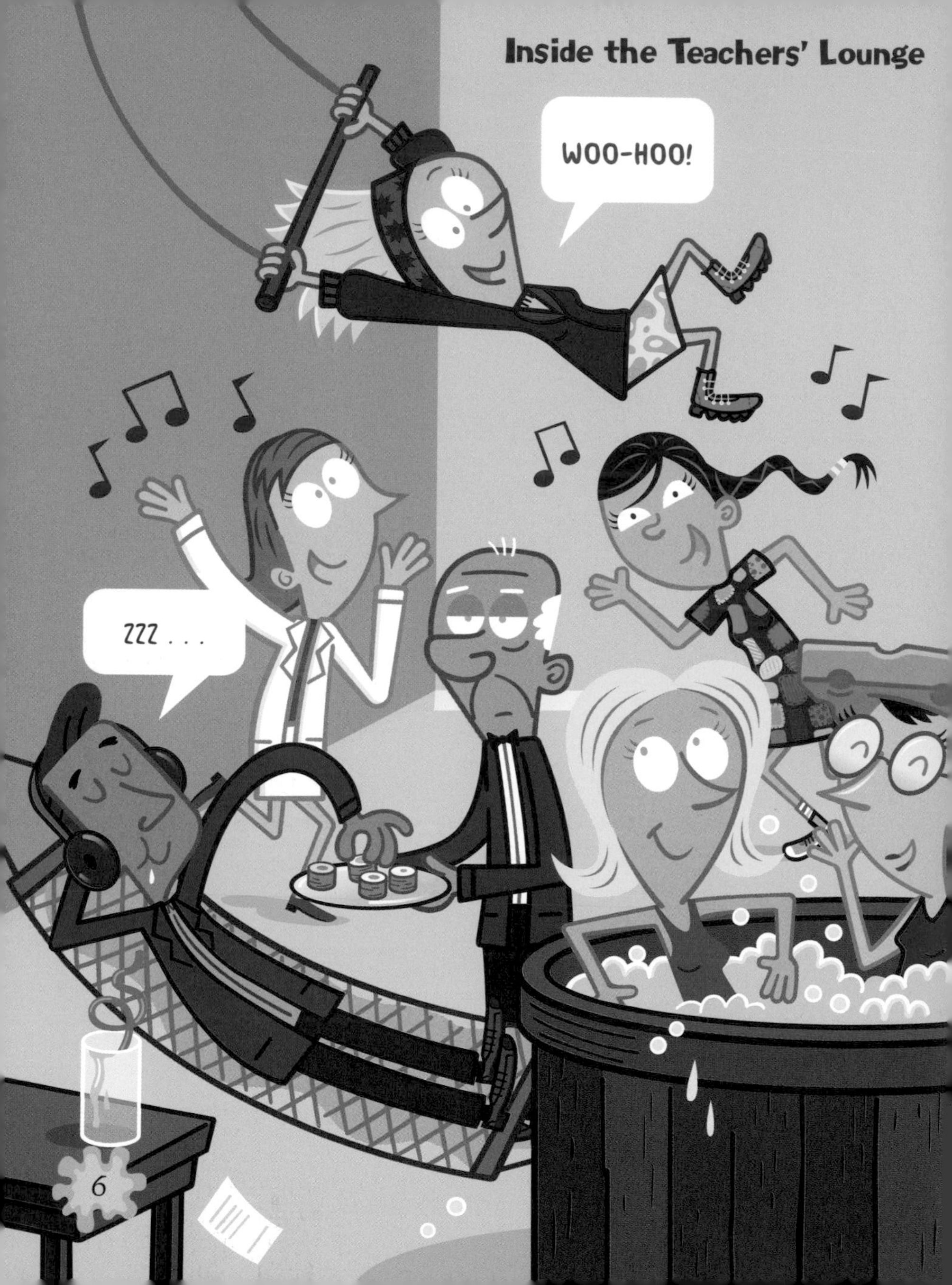
Inside the Teachers' Lounge
WOO-HOO!
ZZZ . . .

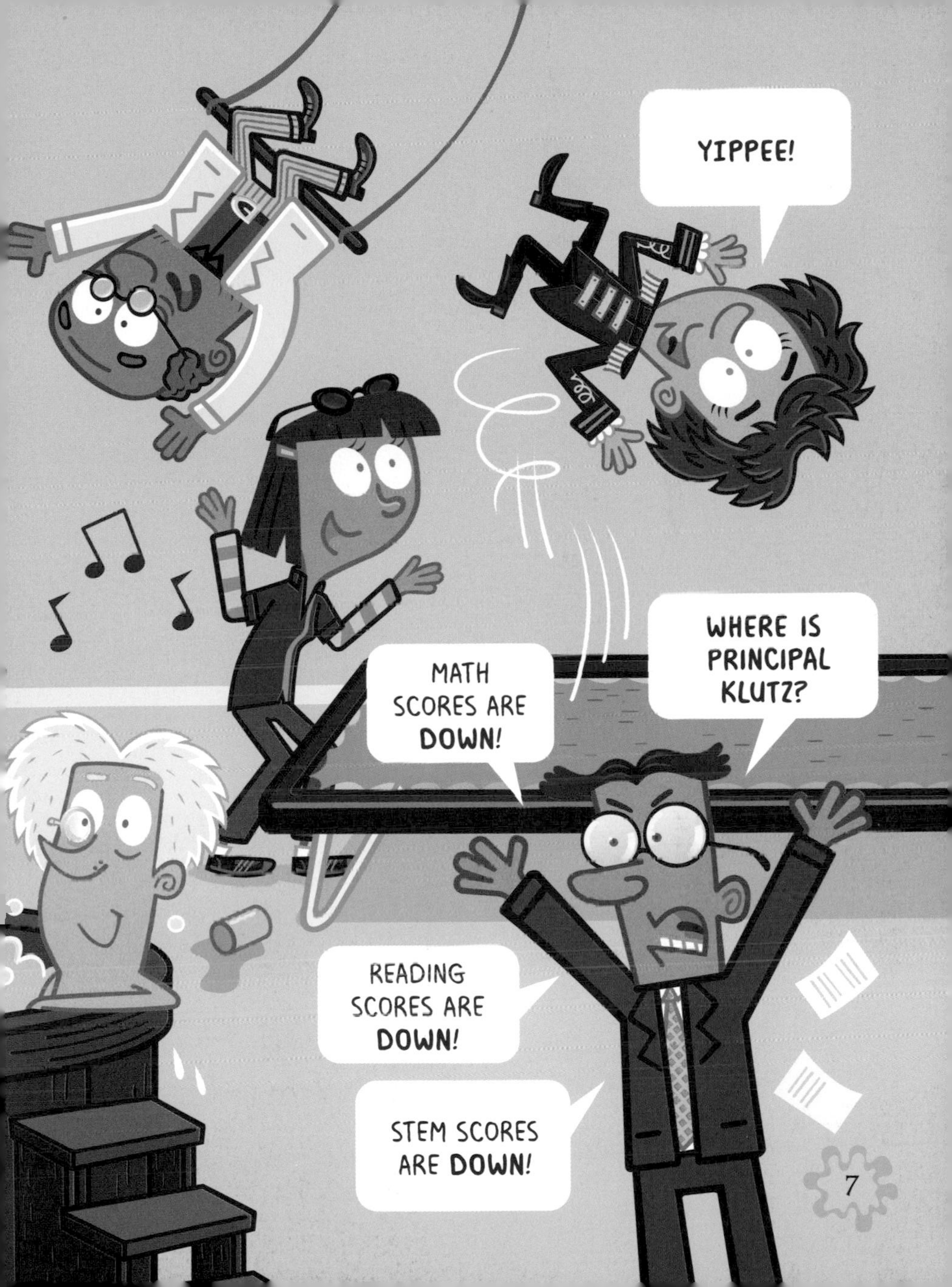
YIPPEE!
MATH SCORES ARE DOWN!
WHERE IS PRINCIPAL KLUTZ?
READING SCORES ARE DOWN!
STEM SCORES ARE DOWN!

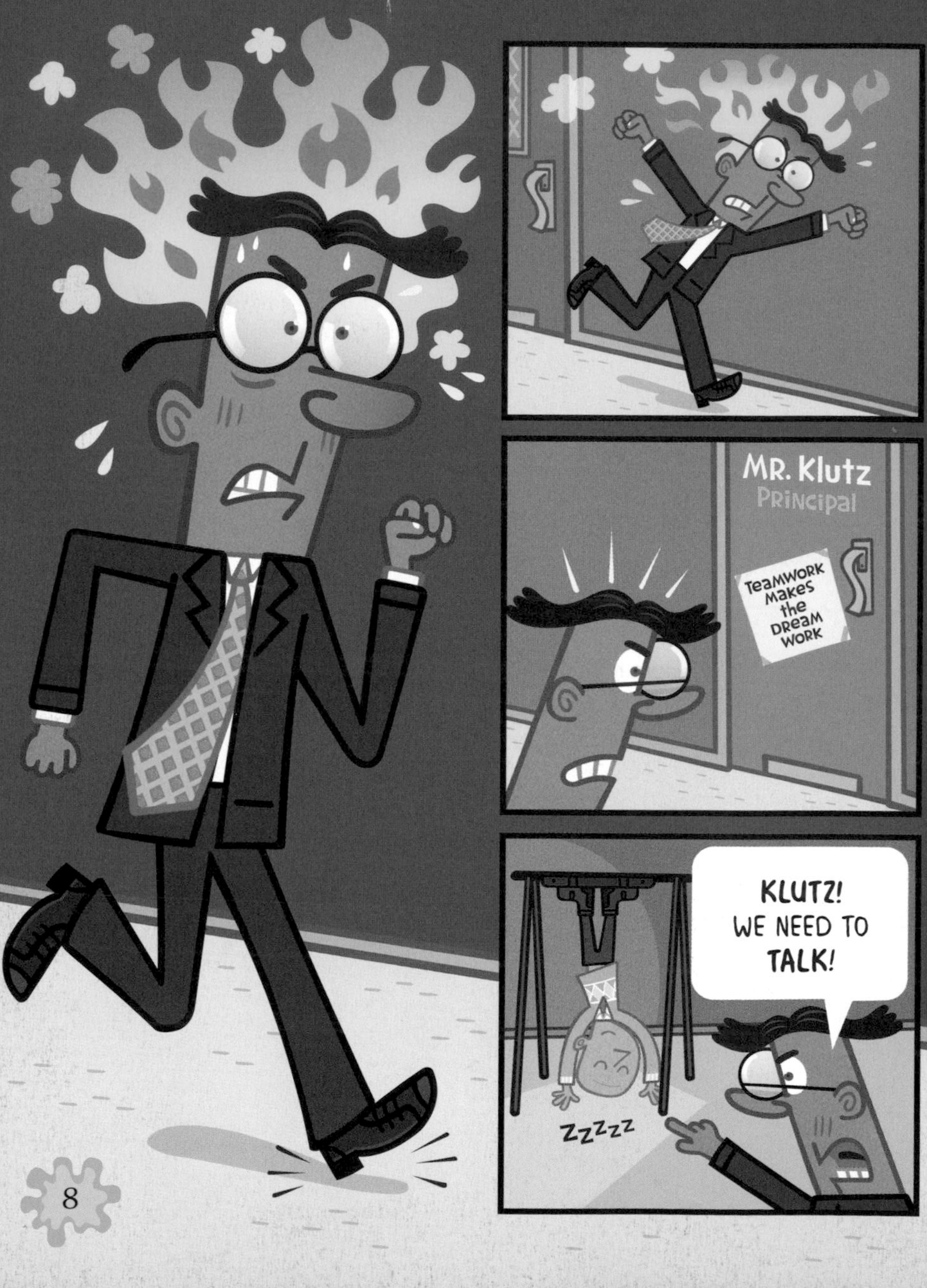
MR. Klutz
Principal
TeaMWORK Makes the DReaM WORK
KLUTZ! WE NEED TO TALK!
ZZZZZ

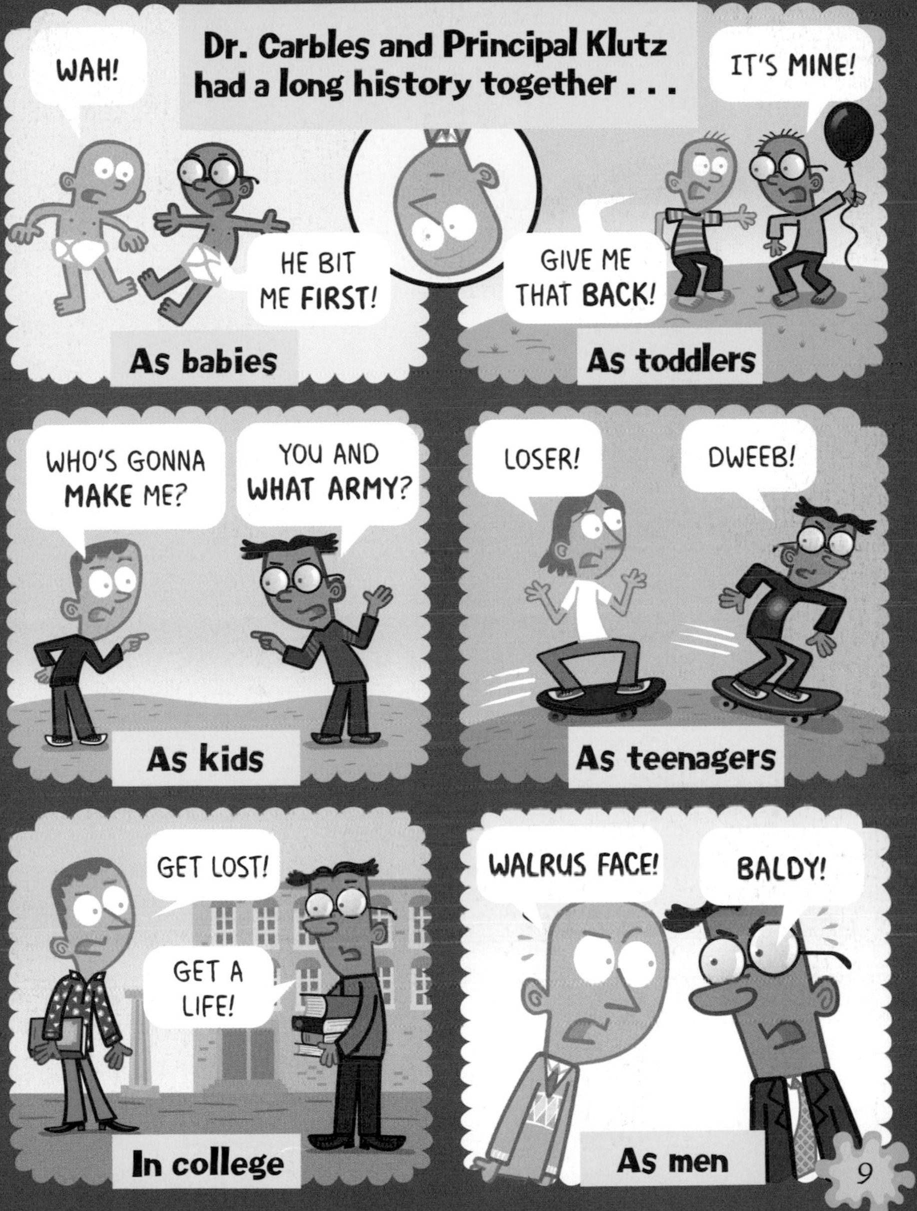
Dr. Carbles and Principal Klutz had a long history together . . .
WAH!
HE BIT ME FIRST!
As babies
IT'S MINE!
GIVE ME THAT BACK!
As toddlers
WHO'S GONNA MAKE ME?
YOU AND WHAT ARMY?
As kids
LOSER!
DWEEB!
As teenagers
GET LOST!
GET A LIFE!
In college
WALRUS FACE!
BALDY!
As men

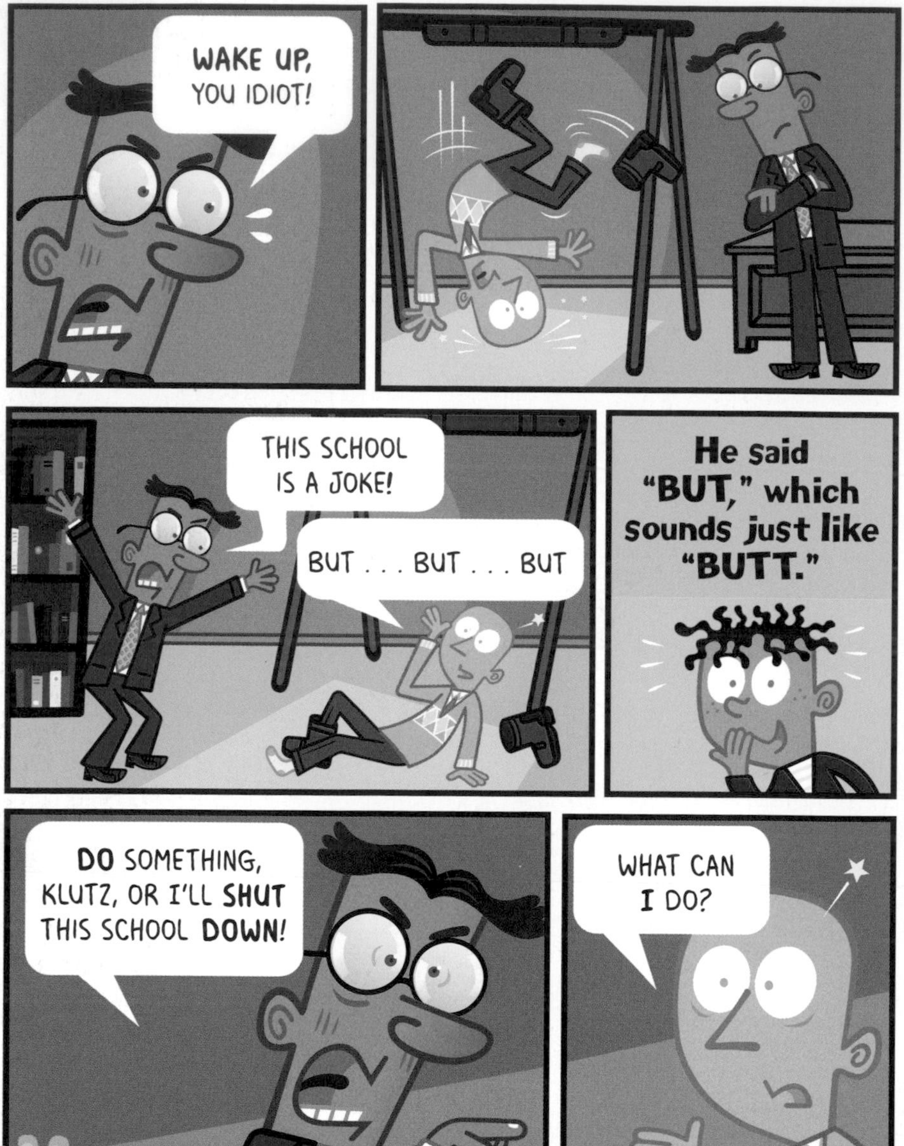
WAKE UP, YOU IDIOT!
THIS SCHOOL IS A JOKE!
BUT . . . BUT . . . BUT
He said "BUT," which sounds just like "BUTT."
DO SOMETHING, KLUTZ, OR I'LL SHUT THIS SCHOOL DOWN!
WHAT CAN I DO?

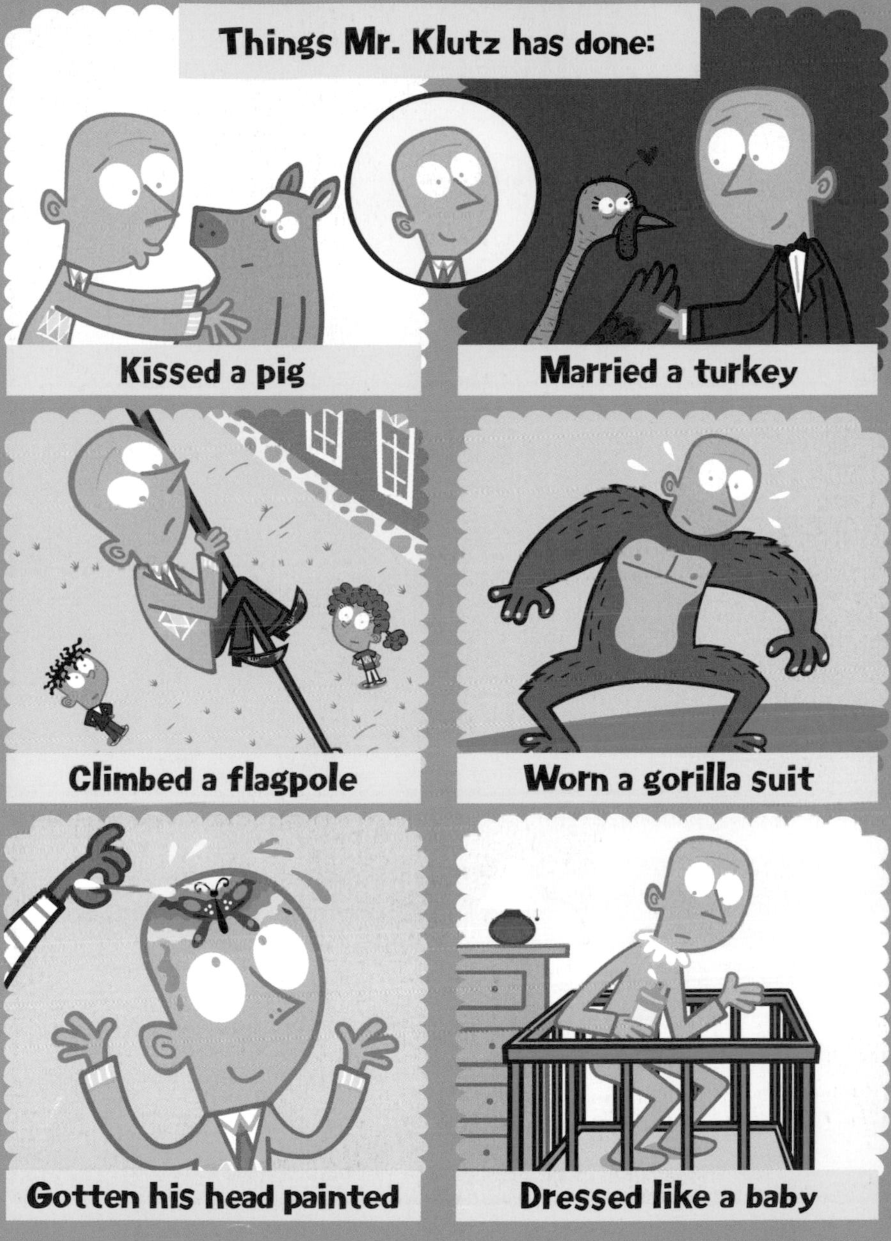
Things Mr. Klutz has done:
Kissed a pig
Married a turkey
Climbed a flagpole
Worn a gorilla suit
Gotten his head painted
Dressed like a baby

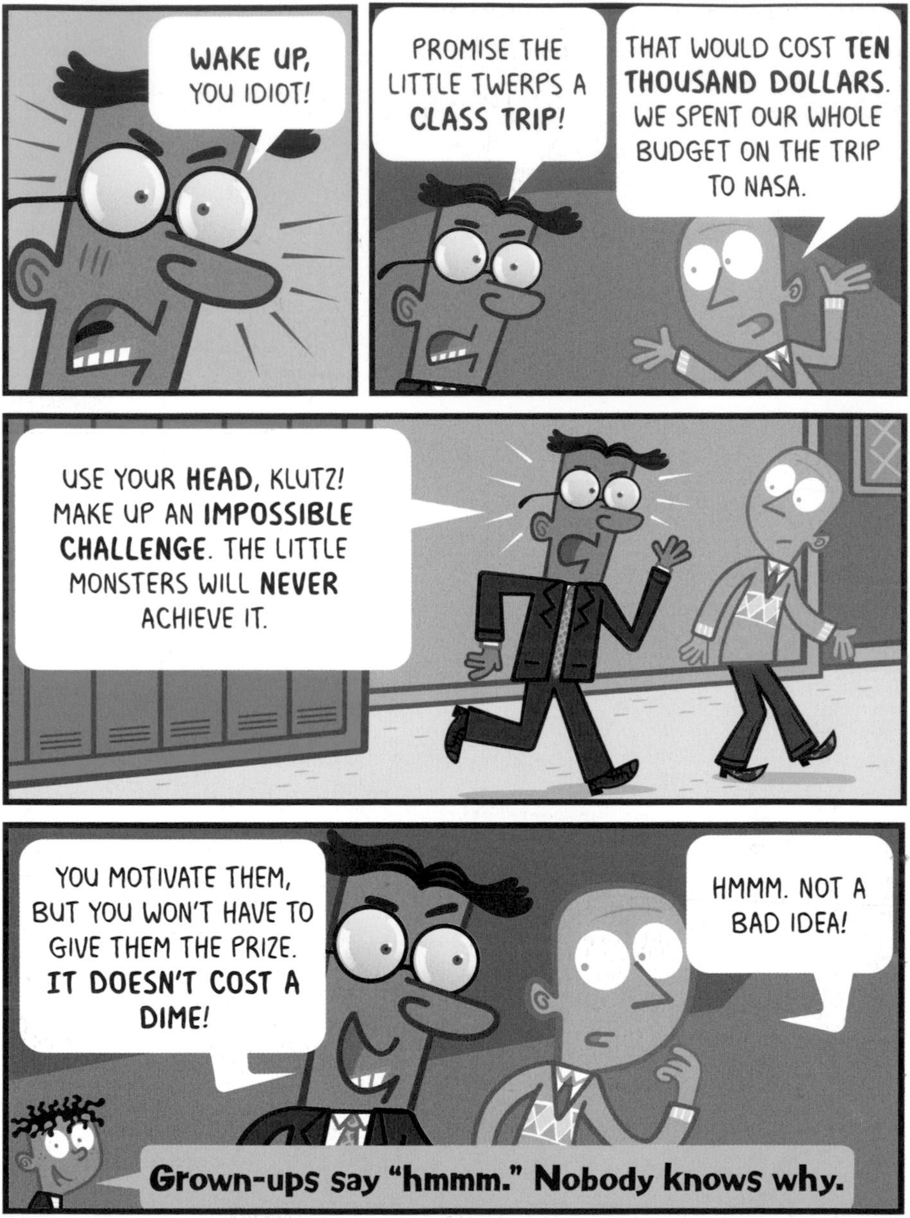
WAKE UP, YOU IDIOT!
PROMISE THE LITTLE TWERPS A CLASS TRIP!
THAT WOULD COST TEN THOUSAND DOLLARS. WE SPENT OUR WHOLE BUDGET ON THE TRIP TO NASA.
USE YOUR HEAD, KLUTZ! MAKE UP AN IMPOSSIBLE CHALLENGE. THE LITTLE MONSTERS WILL NEVER ACHIEVE IT.
YOU MOTIVATE THEM, BUT YOU WON'T HAVE TO GIVE THEM THE PRIZE. IT DOESN'T COST A DIME!
HMMM. NOT A BAD IDEA!
Grown-ups say "hmmm." Nobody knows why.

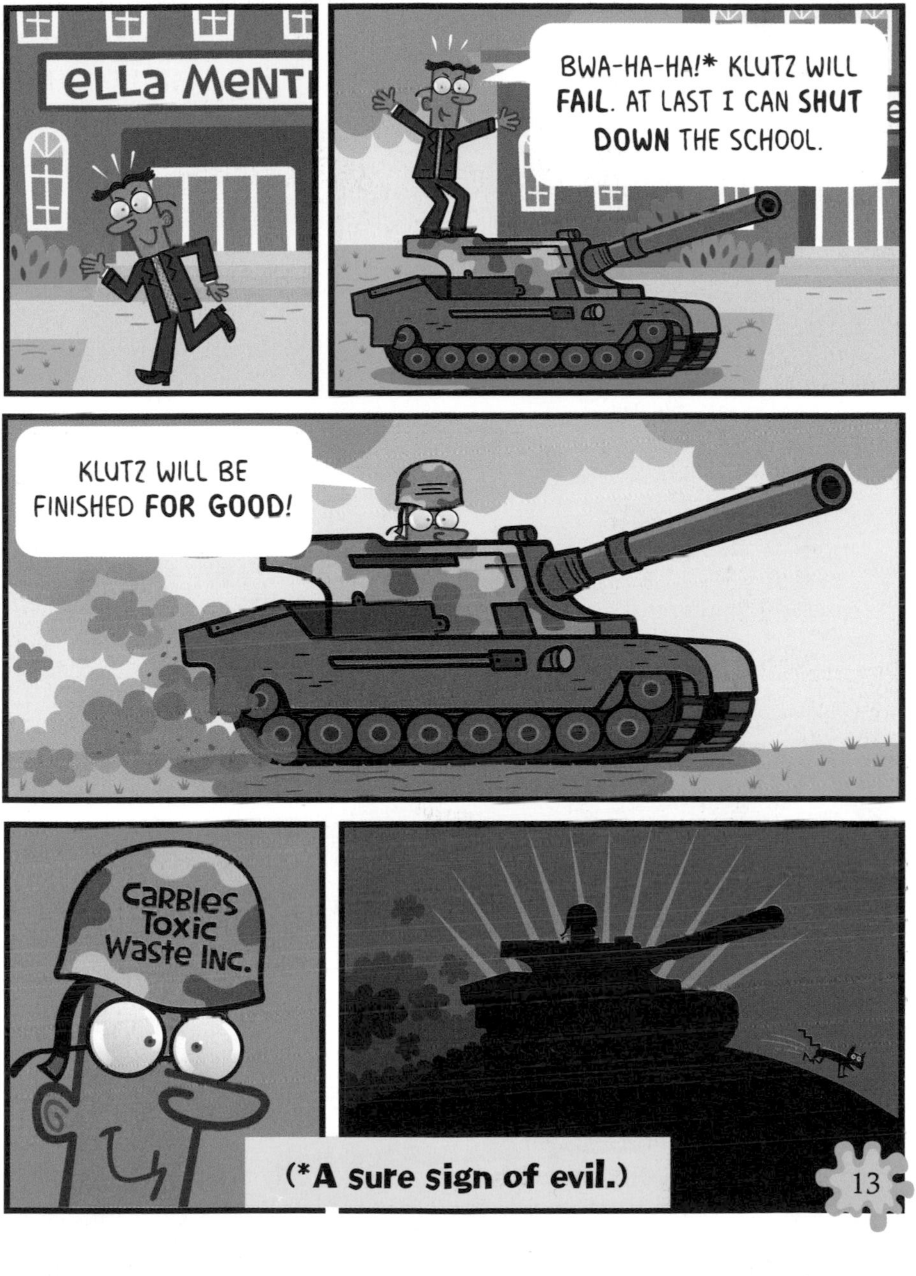

eLLa MENT
BWA-HA-HA!* KLUTZ WILL FAIL. AT LAST I CAN SHUT DOWN THE SCHOOL.
KLUTZ WILL BE FINISHED FOR GOOD!
CaRBles Toxic Waste Inc.
(*A sure sign of evil.)

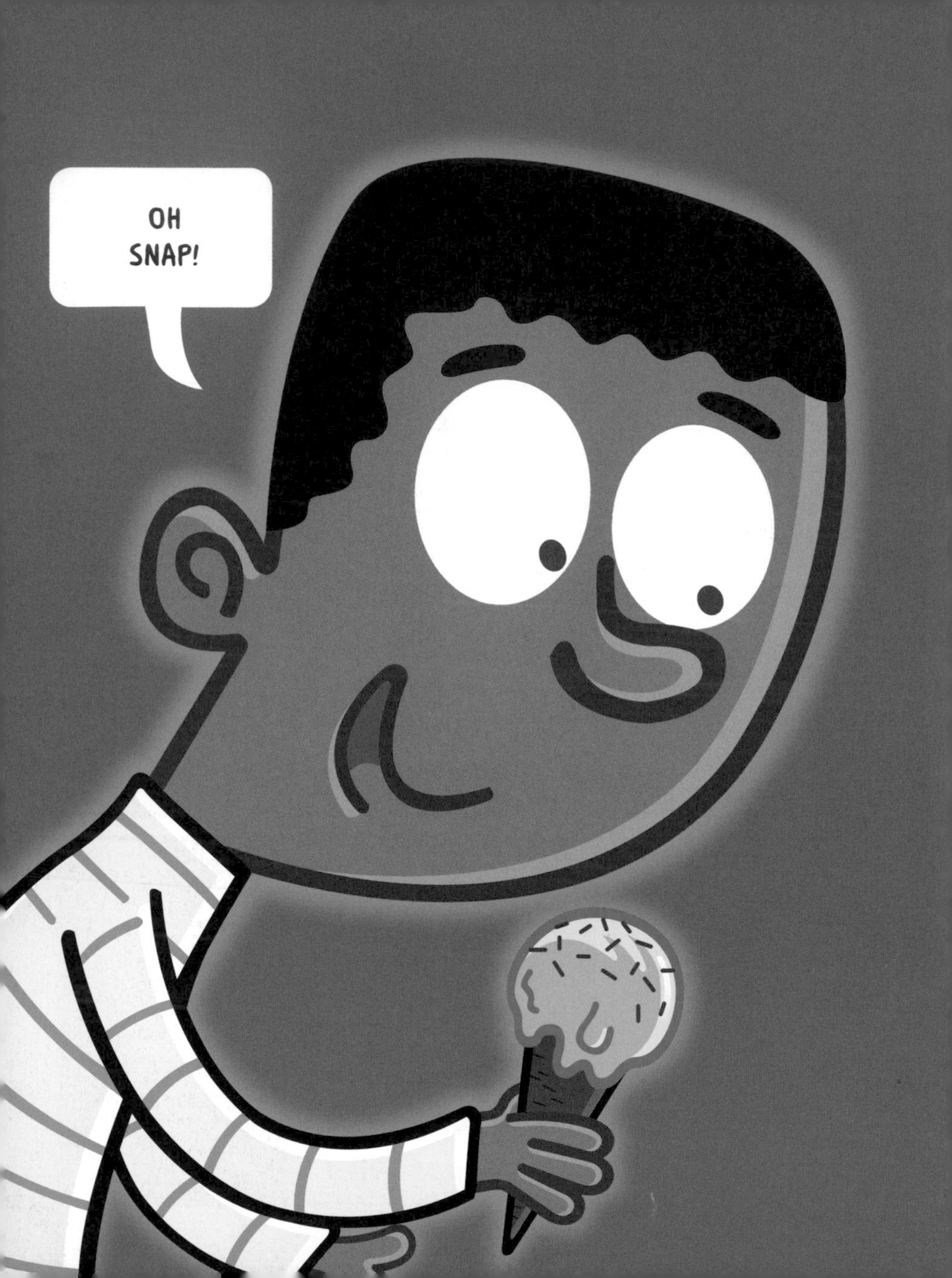
OH SNAP!

CHAPTER 2

More Stuff

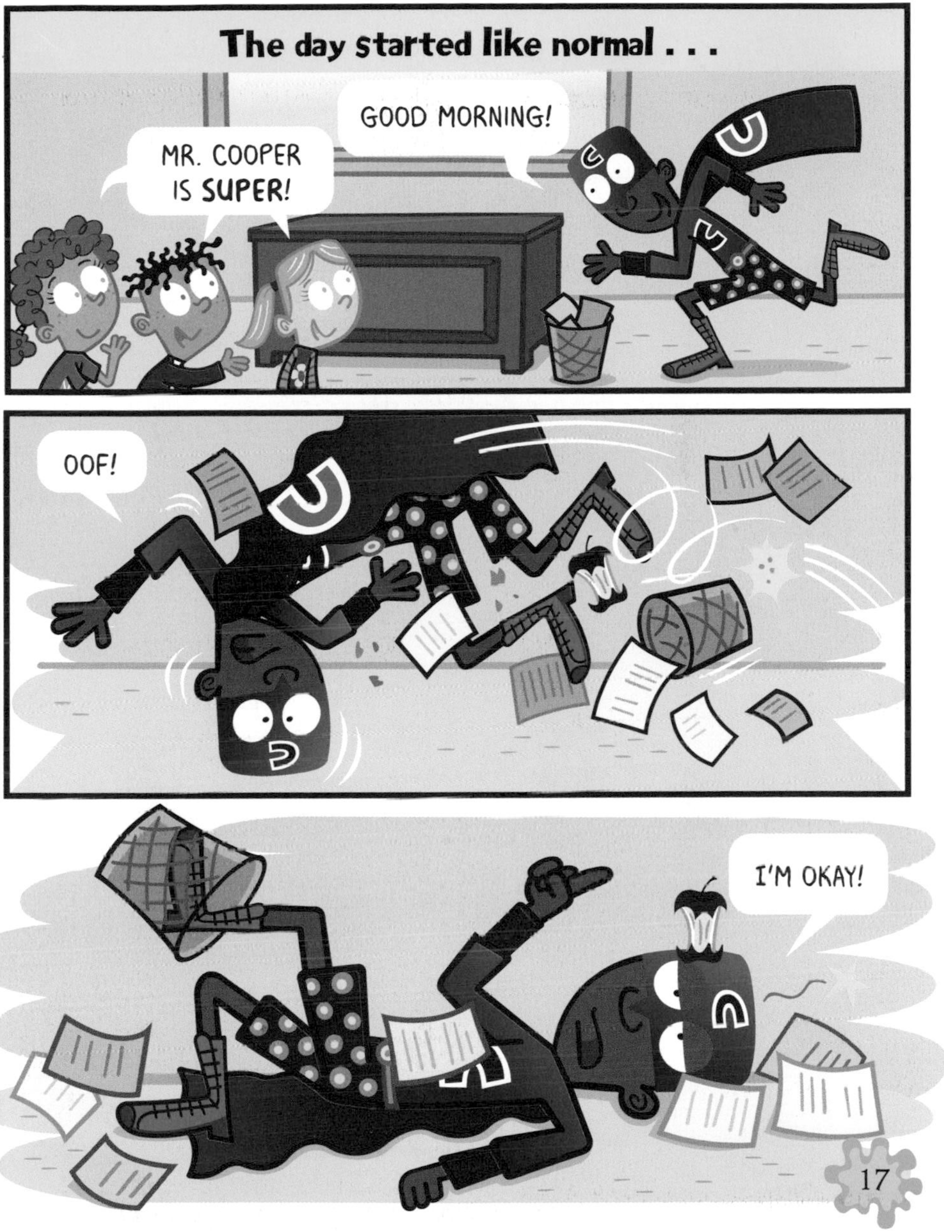
The day started like normal . . .
MR. COOPER IS SUPER!
GOOD MORNING!
OOF!
I'M OKAY!

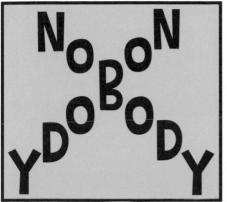

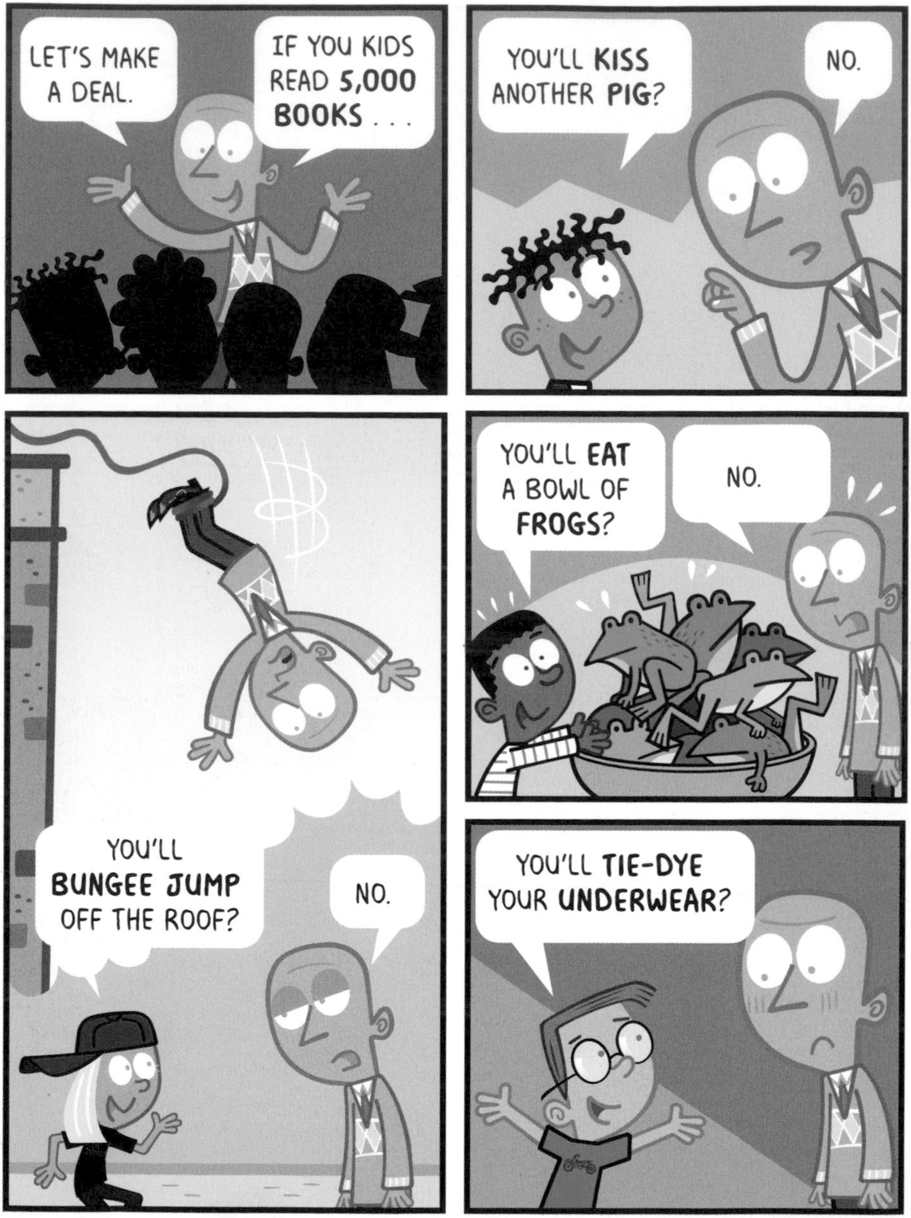
LET'S MAKE A DEAL.
IF YOU KIDS READ **5,000 BOOKS** . . .
YOU'LL **KISS** ANOTHER **PIG**?
NO.
YOU'LL **BUNGEE JUMP** OFF THE ROOF?
NO.
YOU'LL **EAT** A BOWL OF **FROGS**?
NO.
YOU'LL **TIE-DYE** YOUR **UNDERWEAR**?

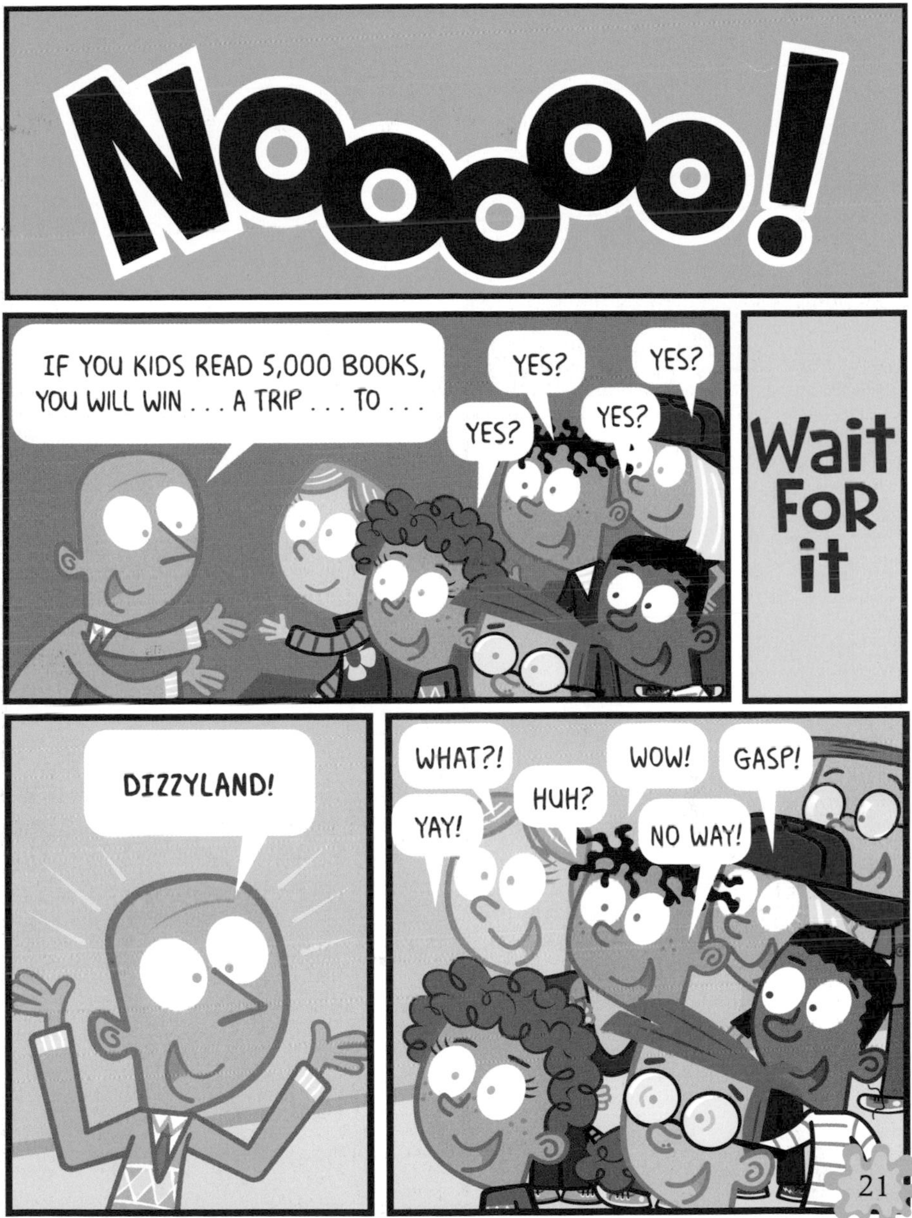
NOOOOOO!
IF YOU KIDS READ 5,000 BOOKS, YOU WILL WIN . . . A TRIP . . . TO . . .
YES?
YES?
YES?
YES?
Wait FOR it
DIZZYLAND!
WHAT?!
YAY!
HUH?
WOW!
NO WAY!
GASP!

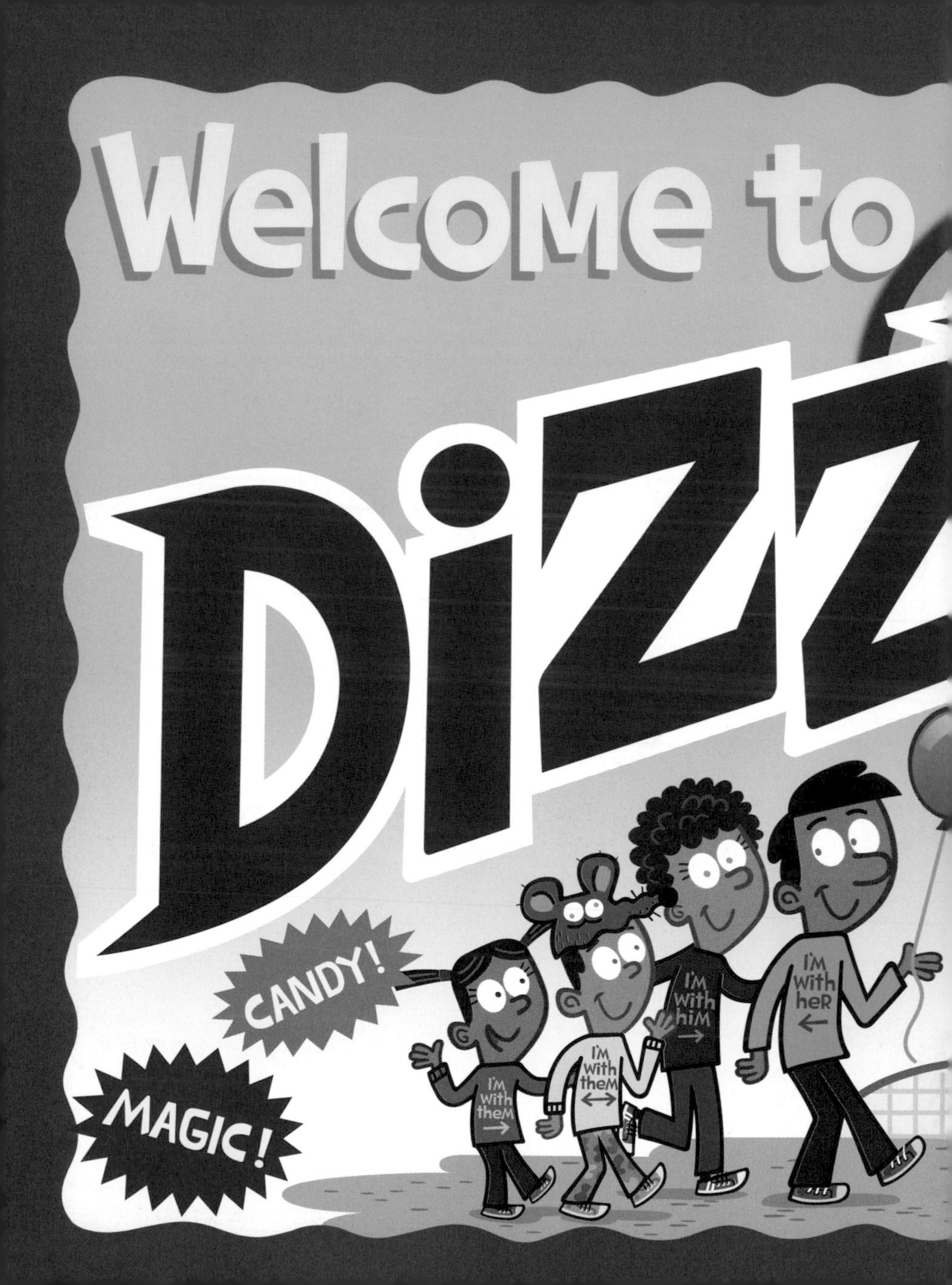

Welcome to
DiZZ
CANDY!
MAGIC!
I'M with theM →
I'M with theM ↔
I'M with hiM →
I'M with heR ←

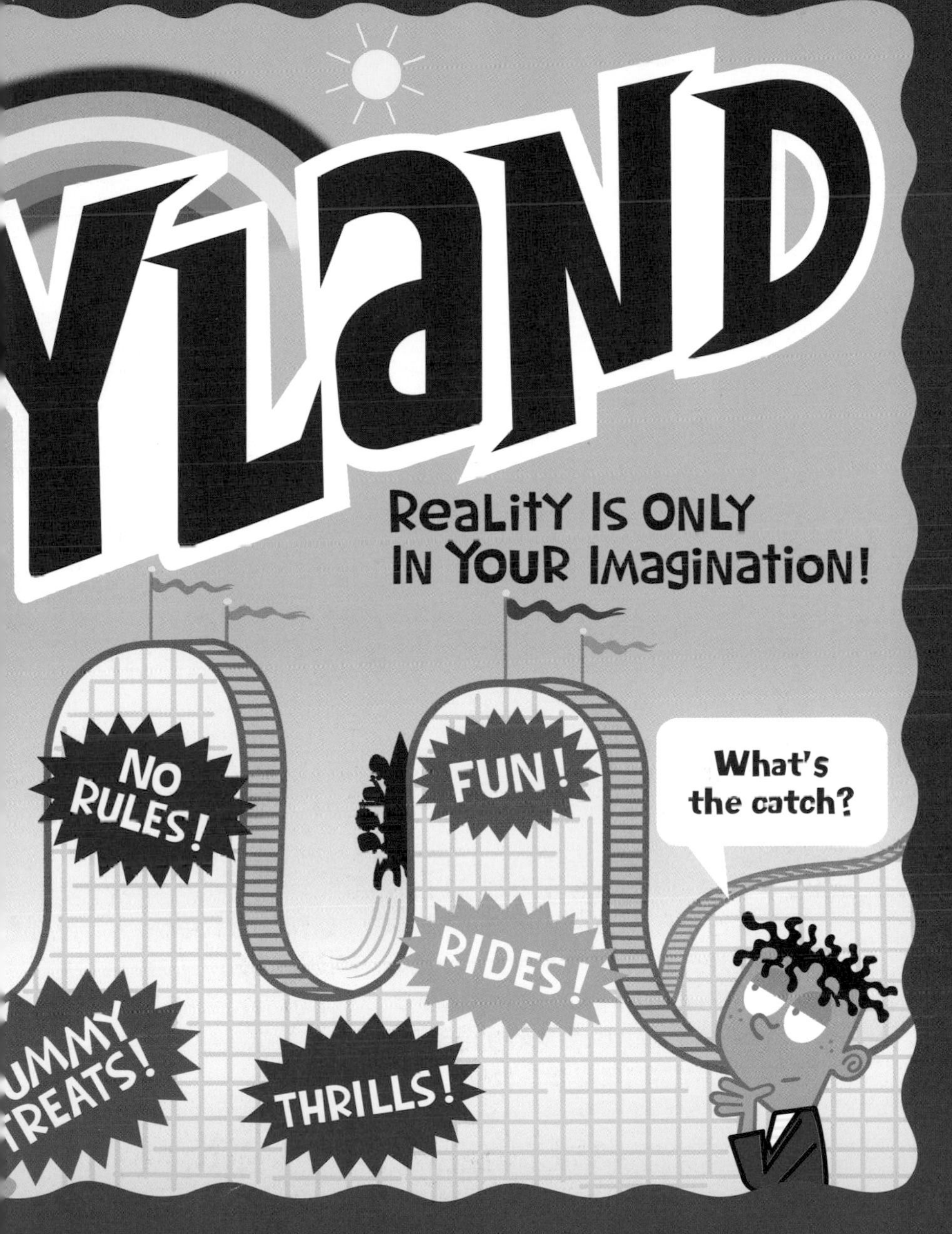
YLAND
ReaLitY Is ONLY
IN YOUR IMagiNatioN!
NO RULES!
FUN!
What's the catch?
RIDES!
UMMY TREATS!
THRILLS!

READER SURVEY

YOUR AGE:

- 0-5
- 6-7
- 9-12
- 13-99
- OVER 100

HOW TALL DO YOU WEIGH?

- 103 FOOT POUNDS
- I'M AS HIGH AS AN ELEPHANT'S EYE
- TALL ENOUGH FOR MY FEET TO REACH THE GROUND
- BOB

HOW MANY MY WEIRD SCHOOL BOOKS HAVE YOU READ?

- NONE. I'M NOT EVEN READING THIS ONE.
- 1-5
- 5-10
- ALL OF THEM
- MY WEIRD WHAT?

HOW DO YOU THINK THIS STORY WILL END?

- THE KIDS WILL READ 5,000 BOOKS AND GO TO DIZZYLAND
- MR. KLUTZ WILL APPEAR IN A SHAMPOO COMMERCIAL
- A.J. AND ANDREA WILL GET MARRIED
- EVERYBODY WILL LIVE HAPPILY EVER AFTER
- EVERYBODY WILL DIE IN A MINE SHAFT EXPLOSION

THINGS YOU COULD DO INSTEAD OF READING THIS BOOK . . .
- CURE CANCER
- SOLVE THE CLIMATE CRISIS
- END ALL WARS
- THE DISHES

WHY DON'T BASKETBALL PLAYERS GO ON VACATIONS?
- HOW SHOULD I KNOW?
- NONE OF YOUR BUSINESS
- WHAT DOES THAT HAVE TO DO WITH ANYTHING?
- I THOUGHT THEY DID
- THEY WOULD BE CALLED FOR TRAVELING

WHAT IS YOUR PET PEEVE?
- PETS
- PEOPLE WHO TALK TOO LOUDLY
- PEOPLE WHO TALK TOO SOFTLY
- PEOPLE WHO ASK ME WHAT MY PET PEEVE IS

TWO TRAINS ARE GOING 100 MPH. TRAIN *A* IS 50 MILES AWAY, AND TRAIN *B* IS 75 MILES AWAY. HOW MUCH SOONER WILL TRAIN *A* ARRIVE?
- WHO CARES?
- I PREFER TO DRIVE
- THOSE ARE DUMB NAMES FOR TRAINS
- BOB

TEAR OUT THIS PAGE AND MAKE IT INTO A PAPER AIRPLANE. THROW IT OUT THE WINDOW. THEN BUY A NEW BOOK TO REPLACE THE ONE YOU RUINED. NEXT, TEAR OUT THE SAME PAGE IN THE SECOND BOOK AND FILL OUT THE SURVEY. APPLY TO WET HAIR AND LATHER WITH A GENTLE MASSAGING MOTION. RINSE AND REPEAT.

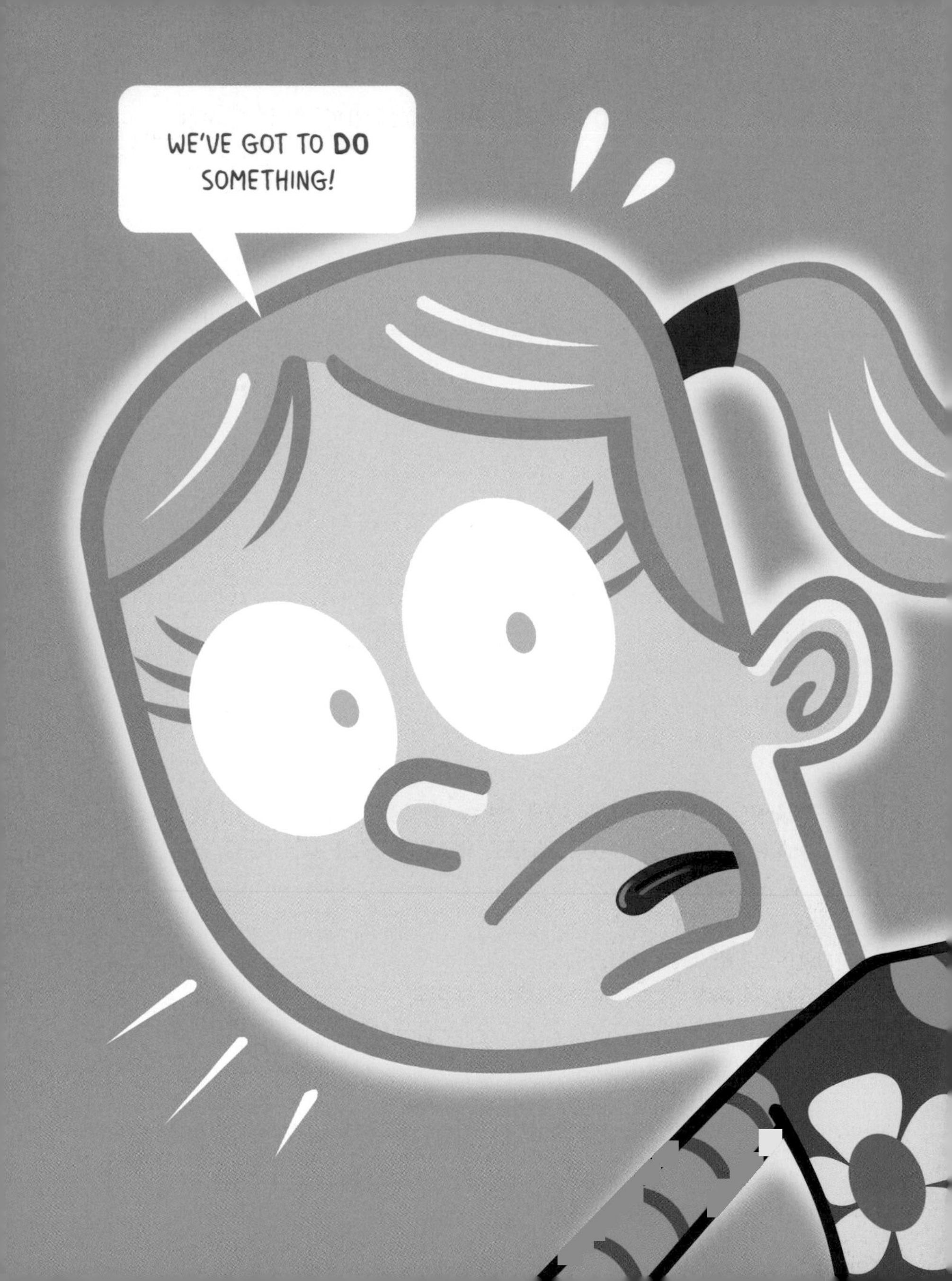
WE'VE GOT TO **DO** SOMETHING!

CHAPTER 3

Even More Stuff

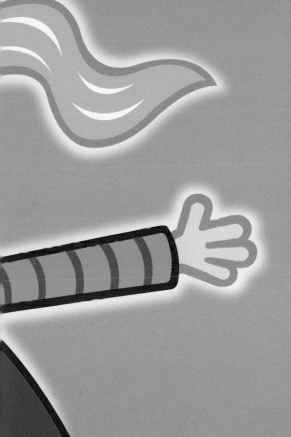

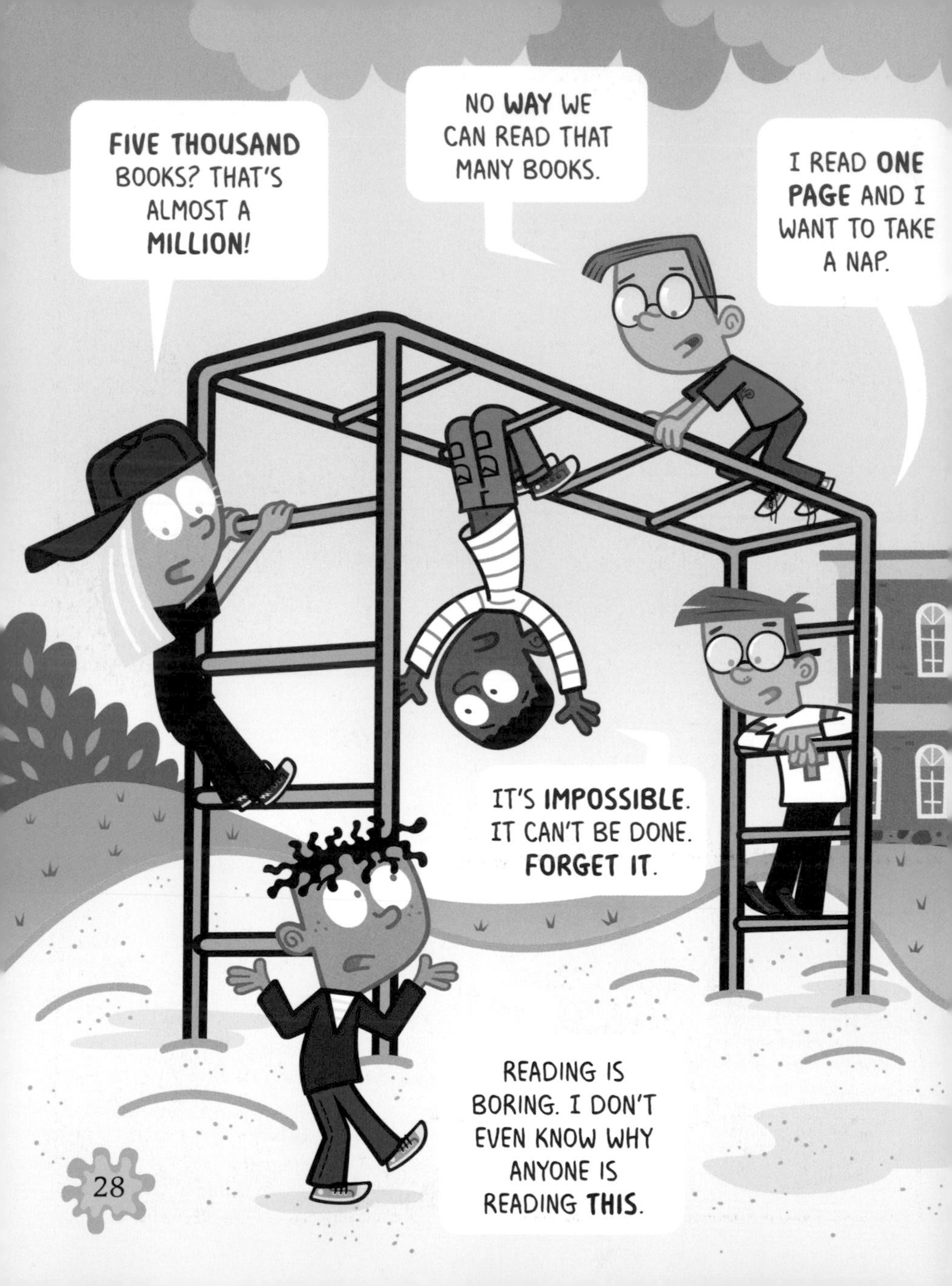
FIVE THOUSAND BOOKS? THAT'S ALMOST A MILLION!
NO WAY WE CAN READ THAT MANY BOOKS.
I READ ONE PAGE AND I WANT TO TAKE A NAP.
IT'S IMPOSSIBLE. IT CAN'T BE DONE. FORGET IT.
READING IS BORING. I DON'T EVEN KNOW WHY ANYONE IS READING THIS.

29

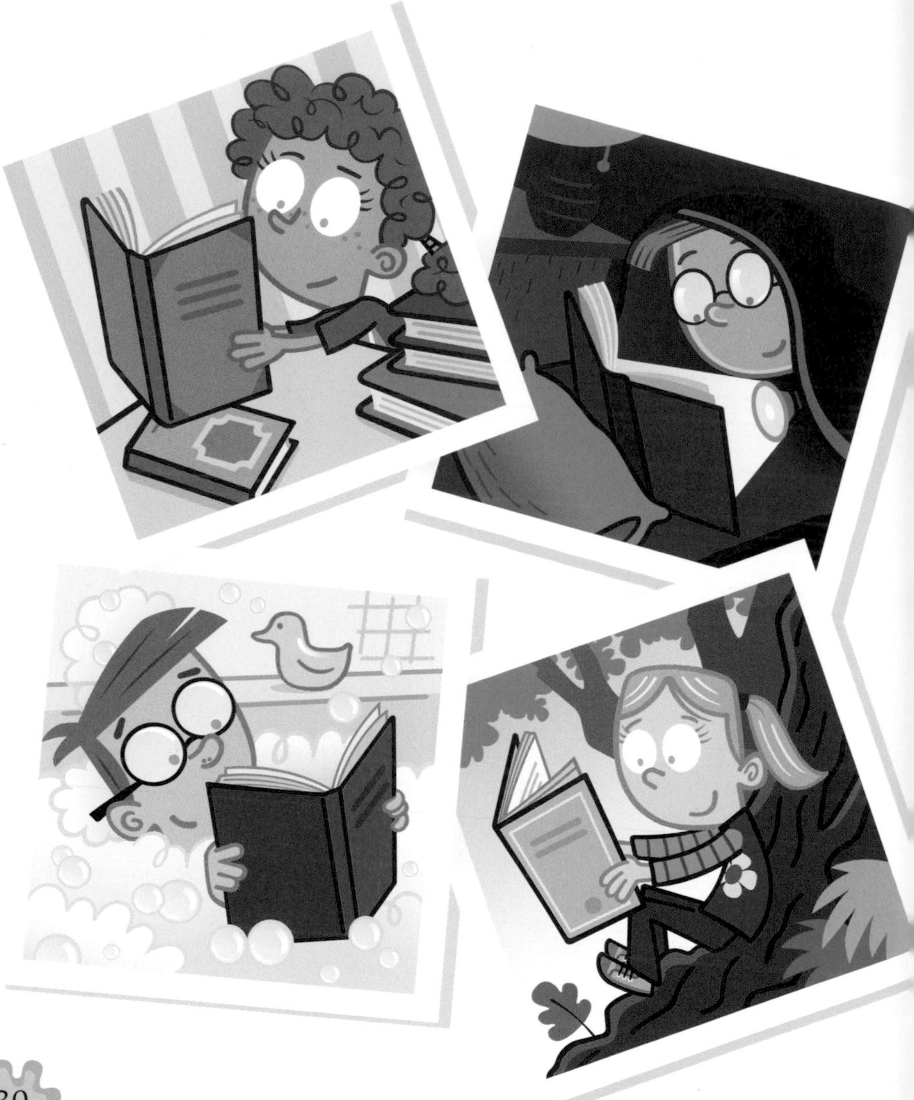

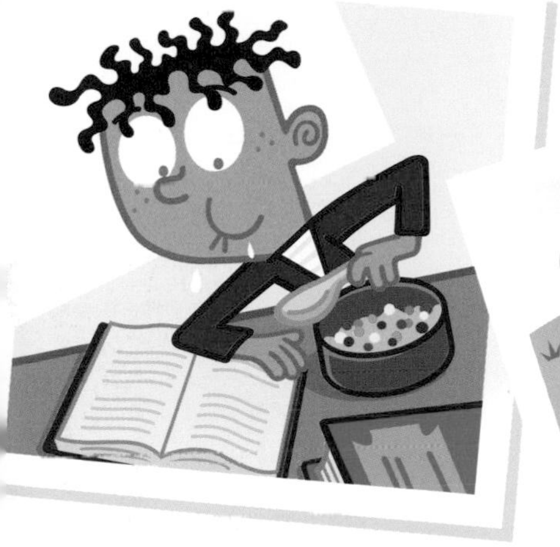
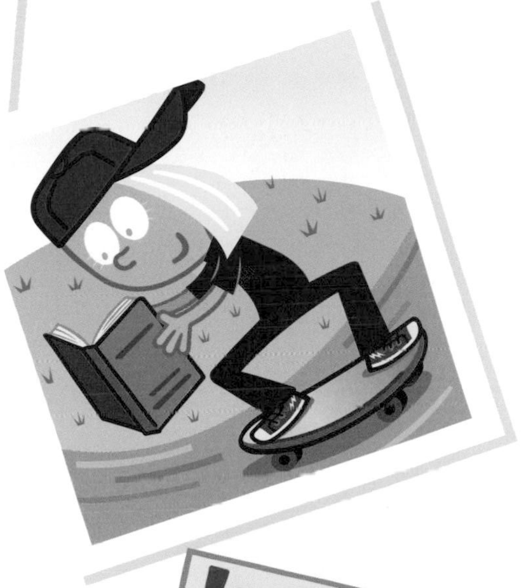
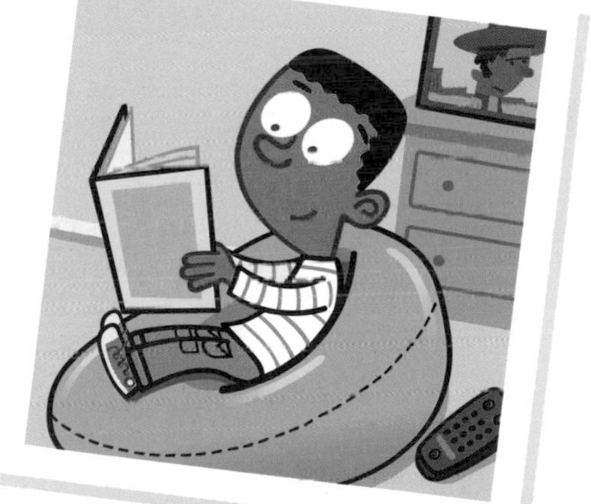
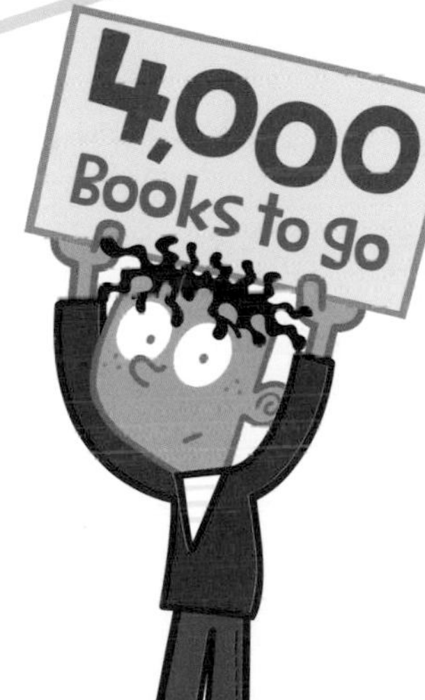
4,000
Books to go

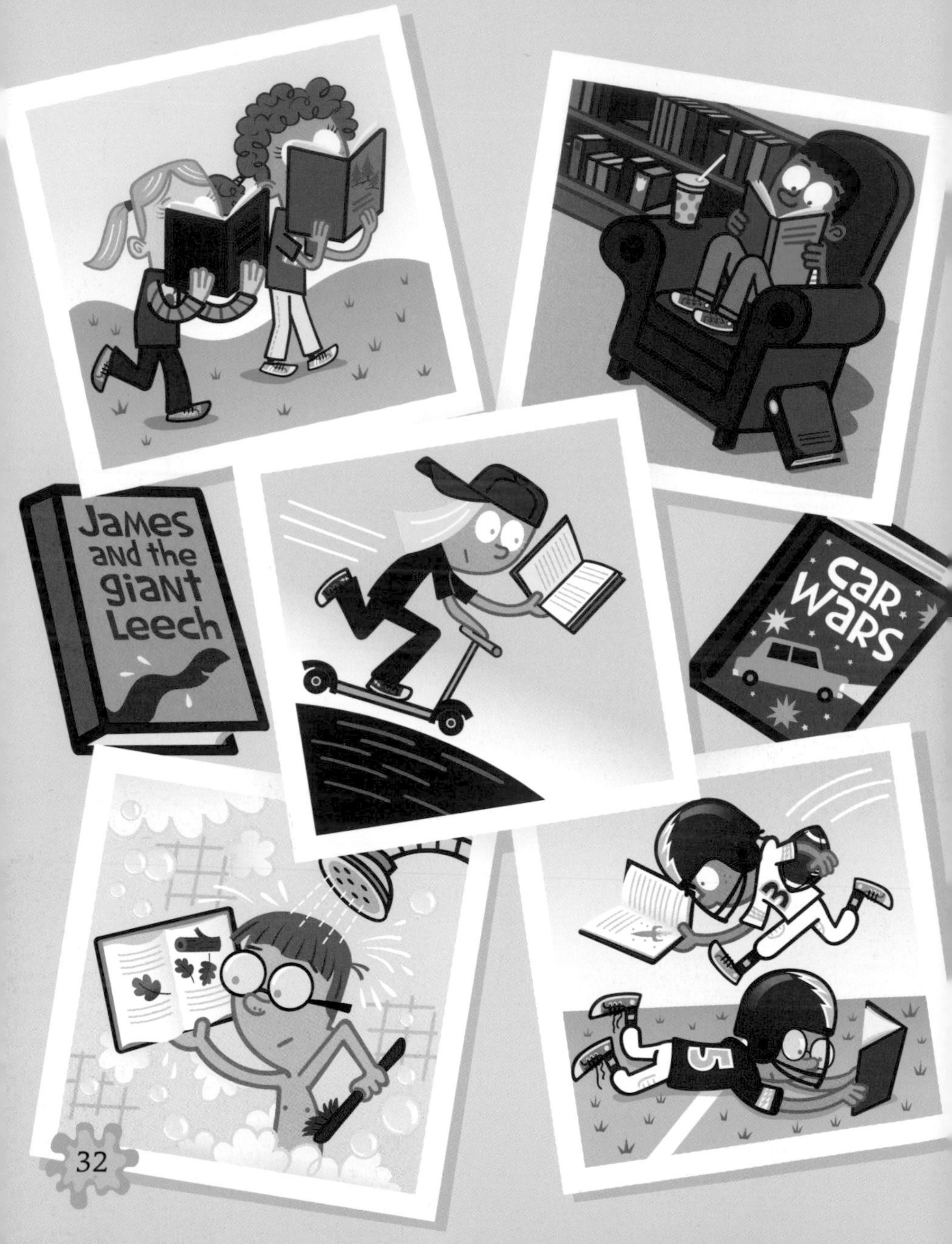
James and the giant Leech
Car Wars
3
5

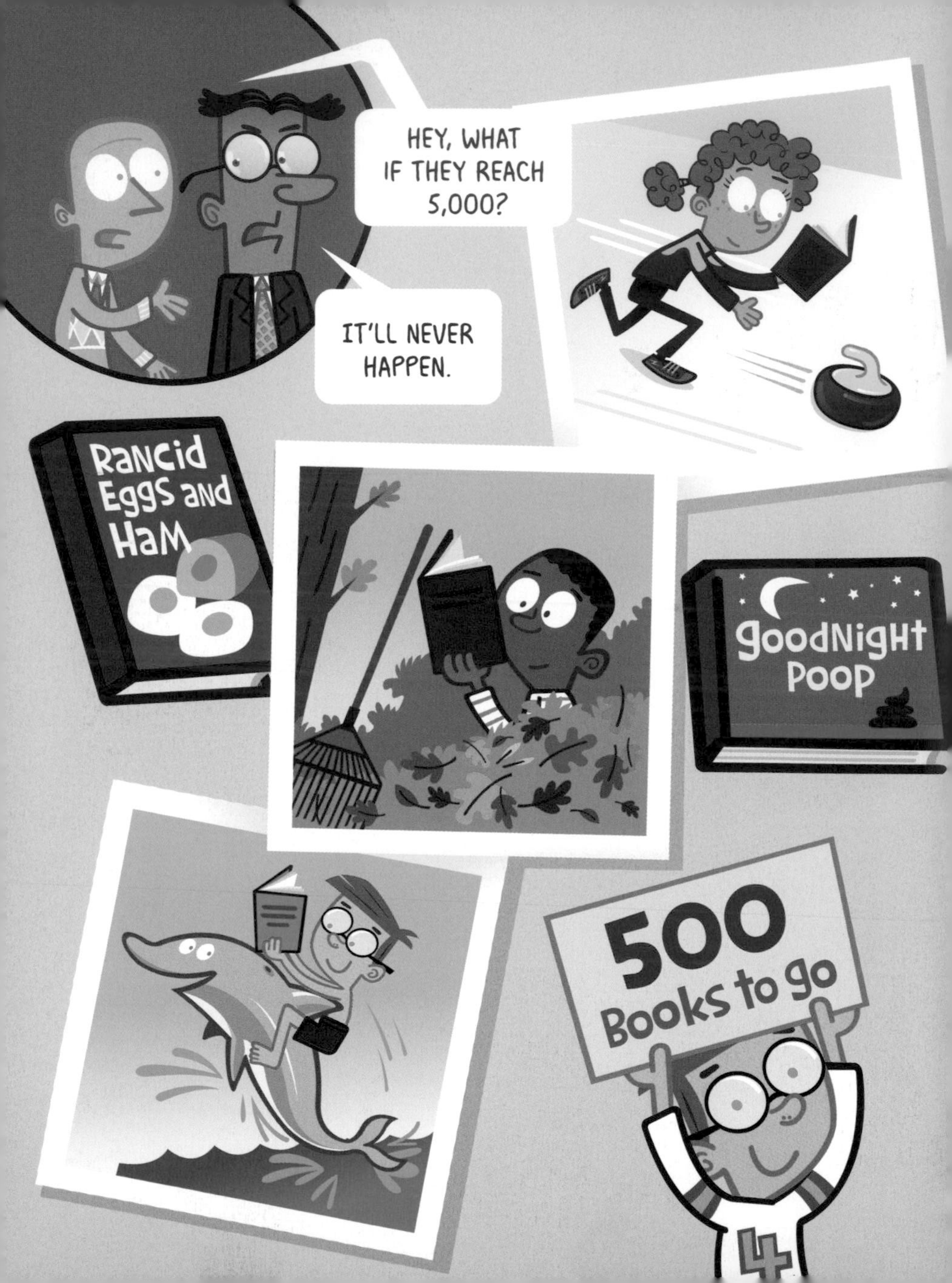
HEY, WHAT IF THEY REACH 5,000?
IT'LL NEVER HAPPEN.
Rancid Eggs and Ham
goodNight Poop
500 Books to go

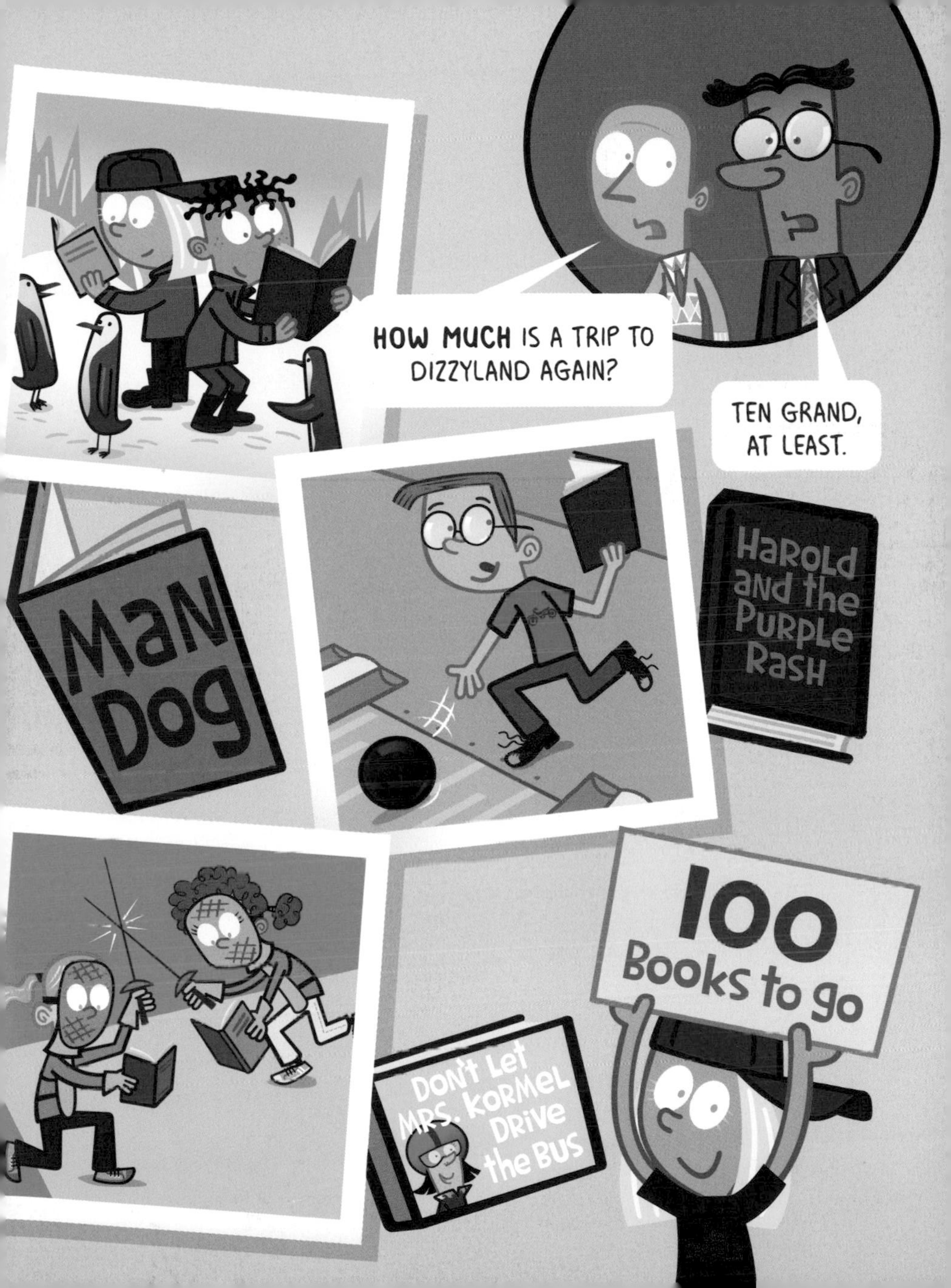
HOW MUCH IS A TRIP TO DIZZYLAND AGAIN?
TEN GRAND, AT LEAST.
MAN DOG
HAROLD AND THE PURPLE RASH
100 Books to go
DON'T LET MRS. KORMEL DRIVE THE BUS

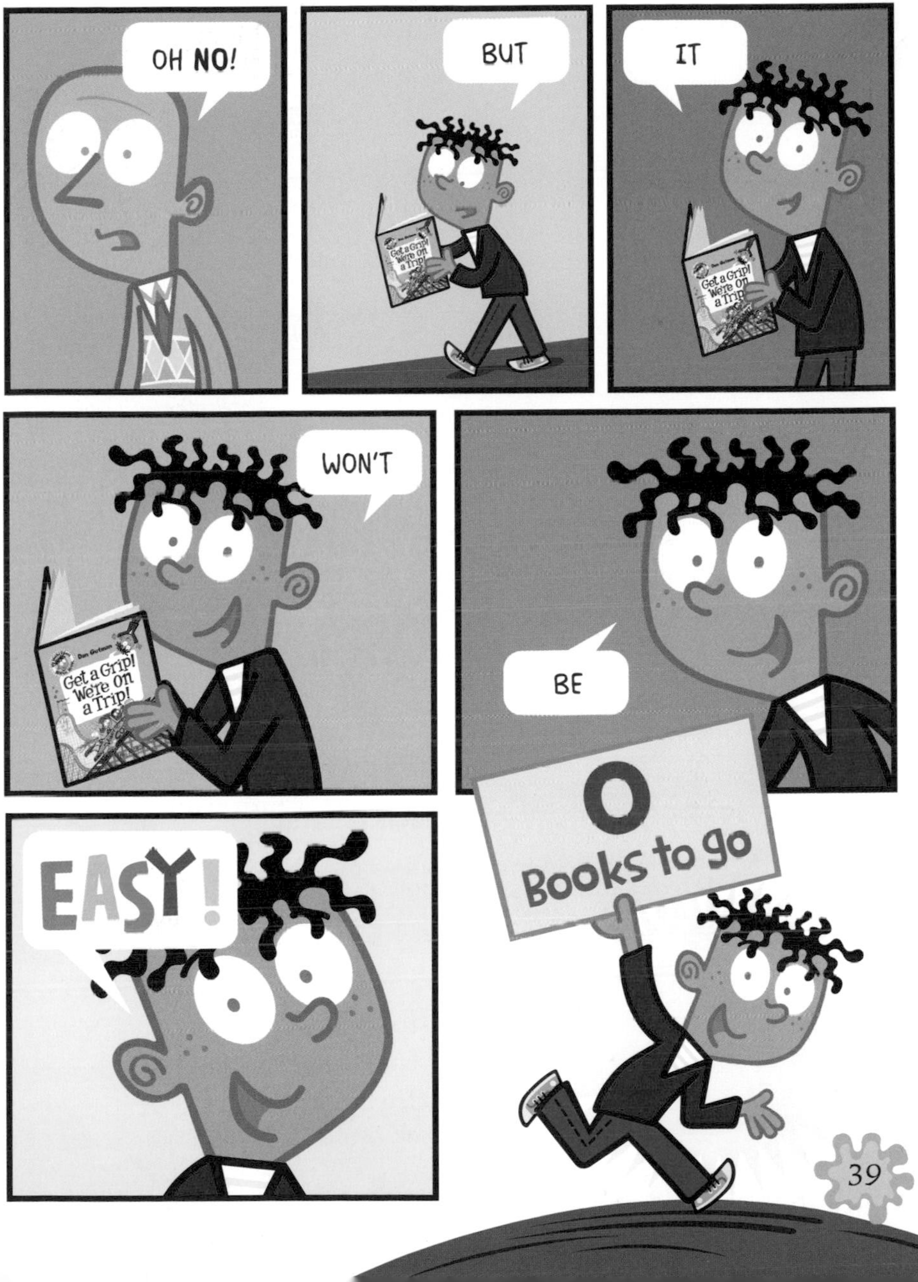
OH NO!
BUT
IT
WON'T
BE
EASY!
0
Books to go

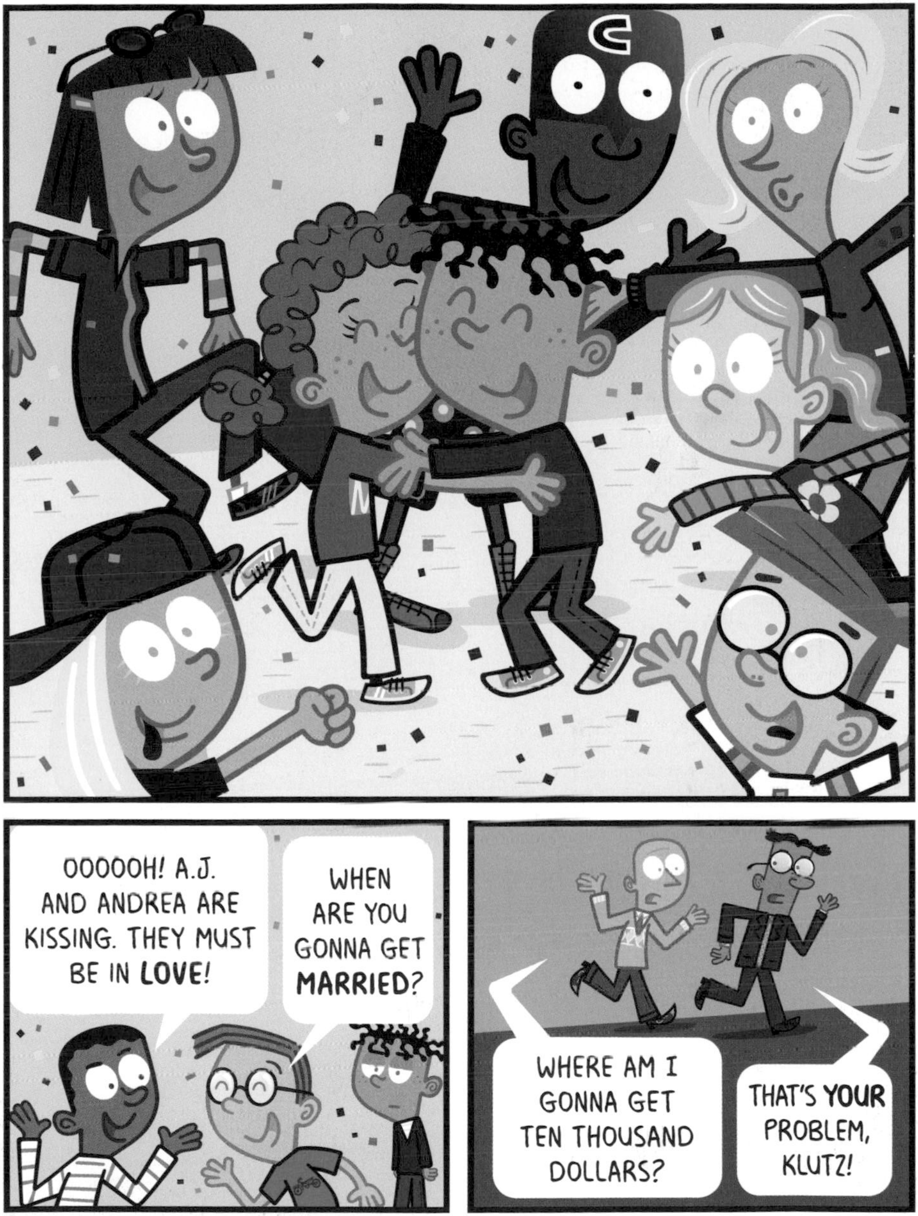
OOOOOH! A.J. AND ANDREA ARE KISSING. THEY MUST BE IN **LOVE**!
WHEN ARE YOU GONNA GET **MARRIED**?
WHERE AM I GONNA GET TEN THOUSAND DOLLARS?
THAT'S **YOUR** PROBLEM, KLUTZ!

WHILE KLUTZ IS AWAY AT DIZZYLAND . . .

I'LL **TEAR DOWN** THE SCHOOL! **BWA-HA-HA!**

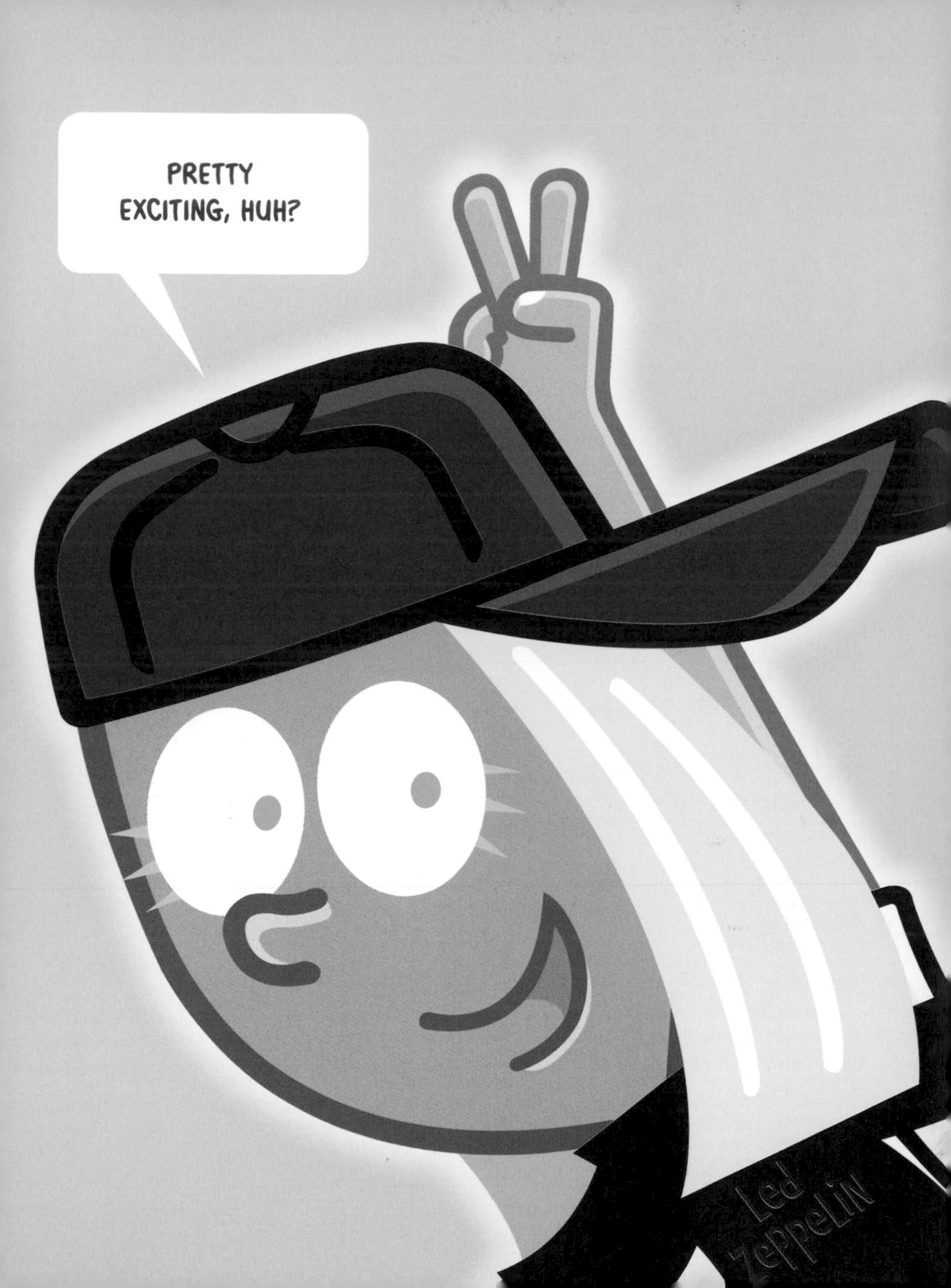
PRETTY EXCITING, HUH?
Led Zeppelin

CHAPTER 4

A Ridorkulous Amount of Stuff

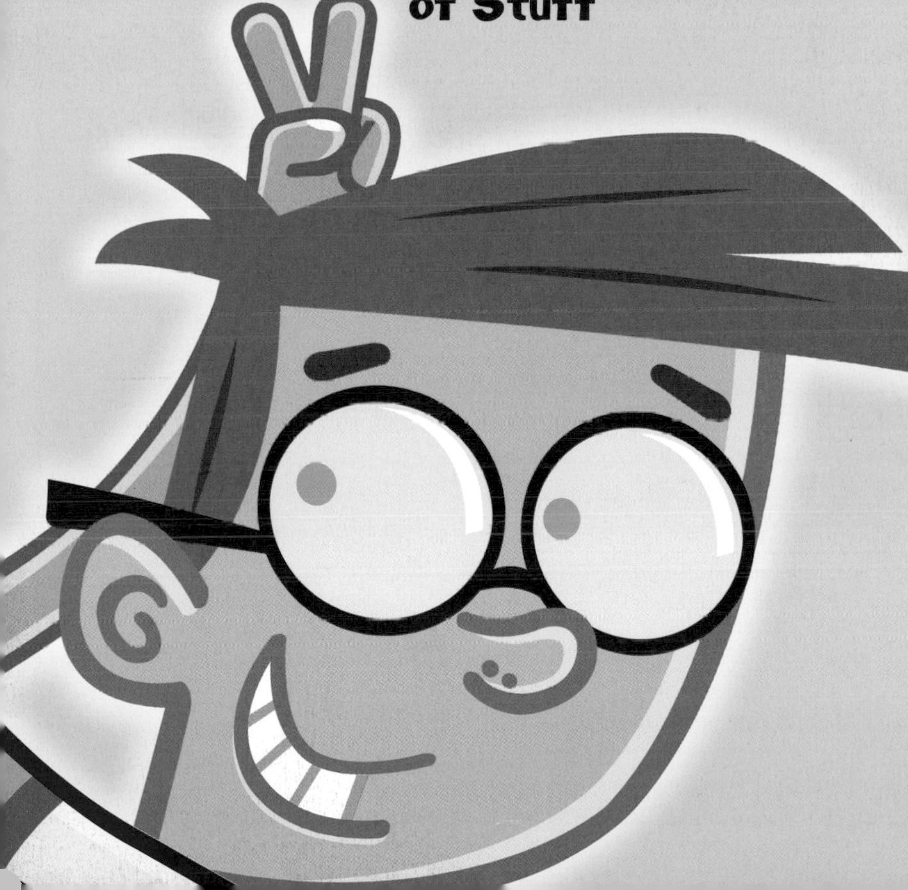

46

47

48

BINGLE BOO!

MRS. KORMEL'S SECRET LANGUAGE

BINGLE BOO = HELLO
LIMPUS KIDOODLE = SIT DOWN
ZINGY ZIP = QUIET DOWN
BIX BLATTINGER = OOOH! BAD WORDS!
NOBODY KNOWS WHAT IT MEANS.

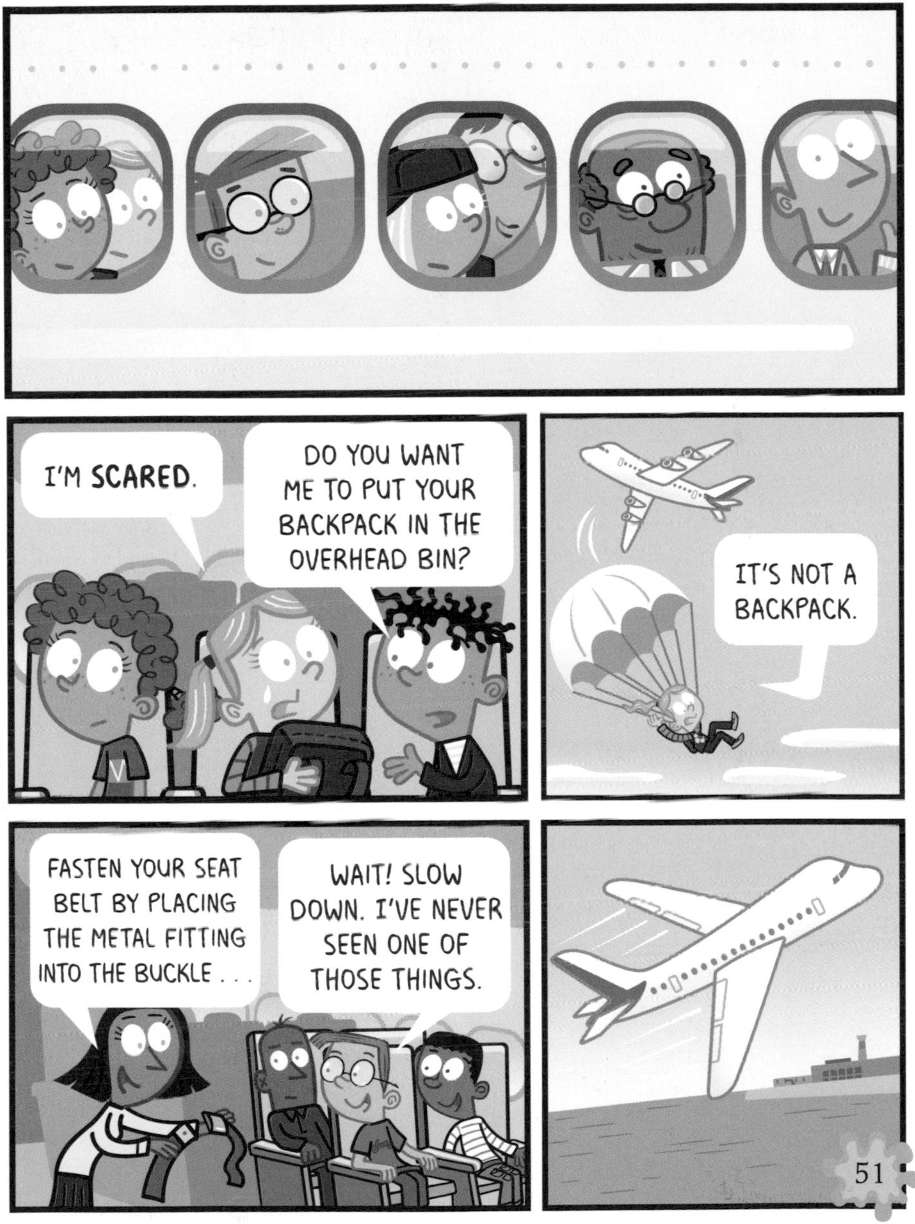
I'M **SCARED**.
DO YOU WANT ME TO PUT YOUR BACKPACK IN THE OVERHEAD BIN?
IT'S NOT A BACKPACK.
FASTEN YOUR SEAT BELT BY PLACING THE METAL FITTING INTO THE BUCKLE . . .
WAIT! SLOW DOWN. I'VE NEVER SEEN ONE OF THOSE THINGS.

The flight took a million hundred hours . . .

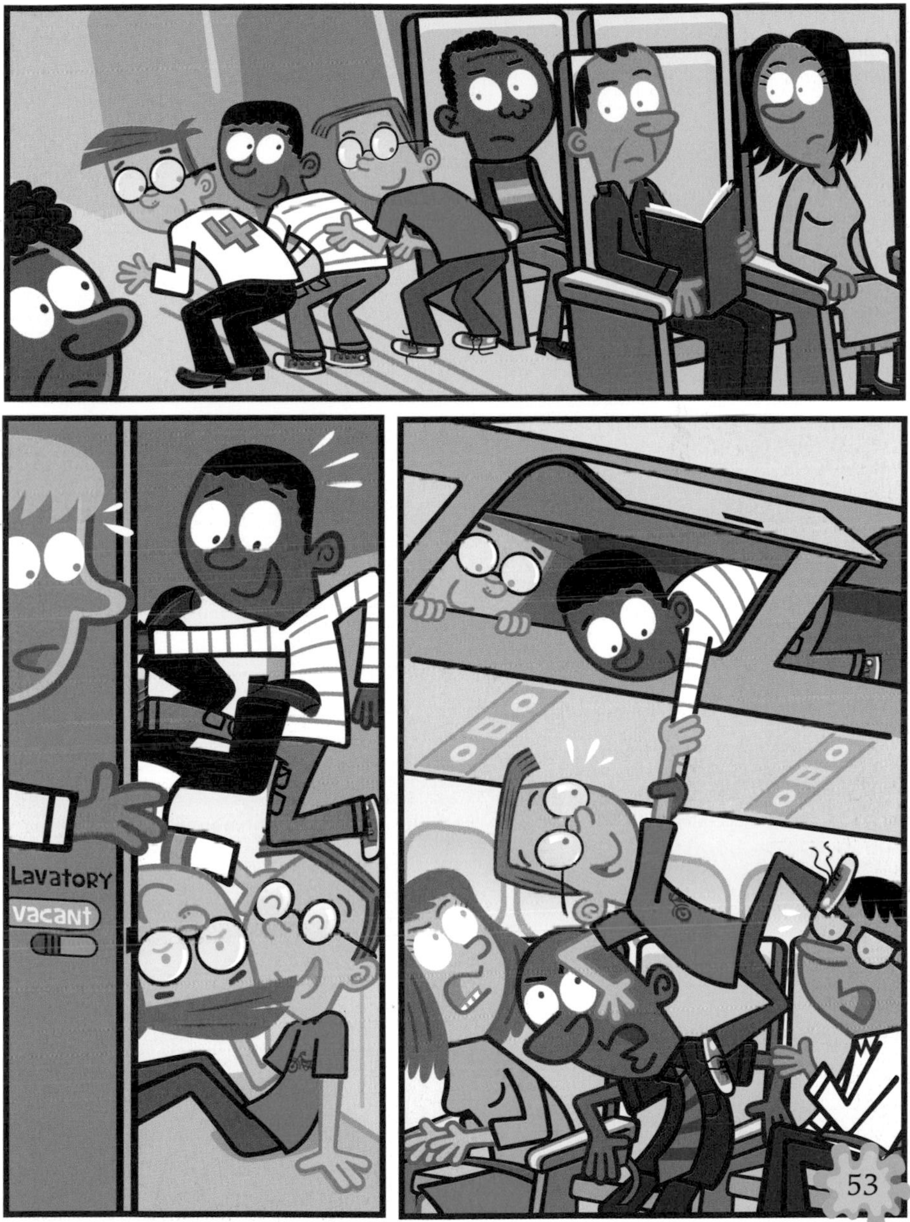
LAVATORY
vacant

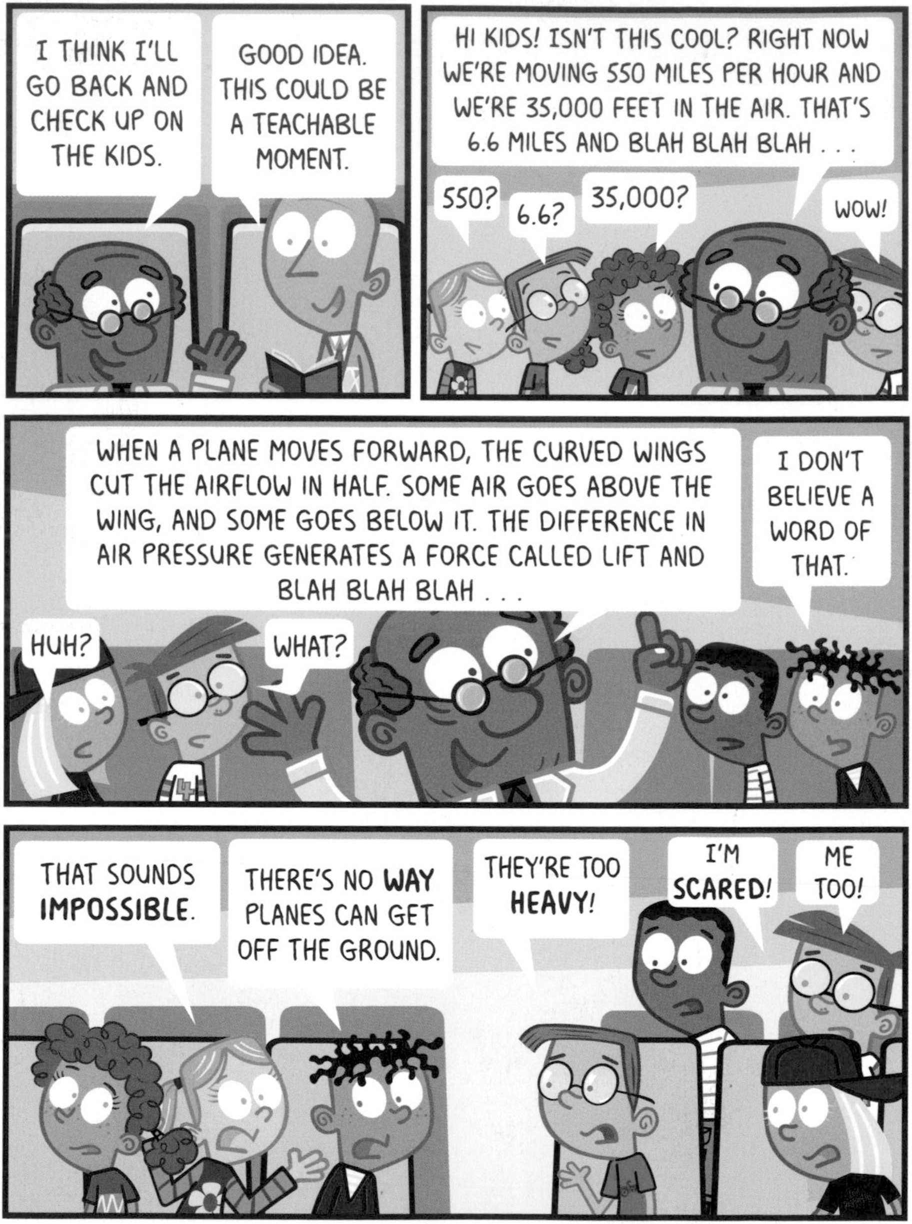

I THINK I'LL GO BACK AND CHECK UP ON THE KIDS.
GOOD IDEA. THIS COULD BE A TEACHABLE MOMENT.
HI KIDS! ISN'T THIS COOL? RIGHT NOW WE'RE MOVING 550 MILES PER HOUR AND WE'RE 35,000 FEET IN THE AIR. THAT'S 6.6 MILES AND BLAH BLAH BLAH . . .
550?
6.6?
35,000?
WOW!
WHEN A PLANE MOVES FORWARD, THE CURVED WINGS CUT THE AIRFLOW IN HALF. SOME AIR GOES ABOVE THE WING, AND SOME GOES BELOW IT. THE DIFFERENCE IN AIR PRESSURE GENERATES A FORCE CALLED LIFT AND BLAH BLAH BLAH . . .
I DON'T BELIEVE A WORD OF THAT.
HUH?
WHAT?
THAT SOUNDS **IMPOSSIBLE**.
THERE'S NO **WAY** PLANES CAN GET OFF THE GROUND.
THEY'RE TOO **HEAVY**!
I'M **SCARED**!
ME TOO!

55

57

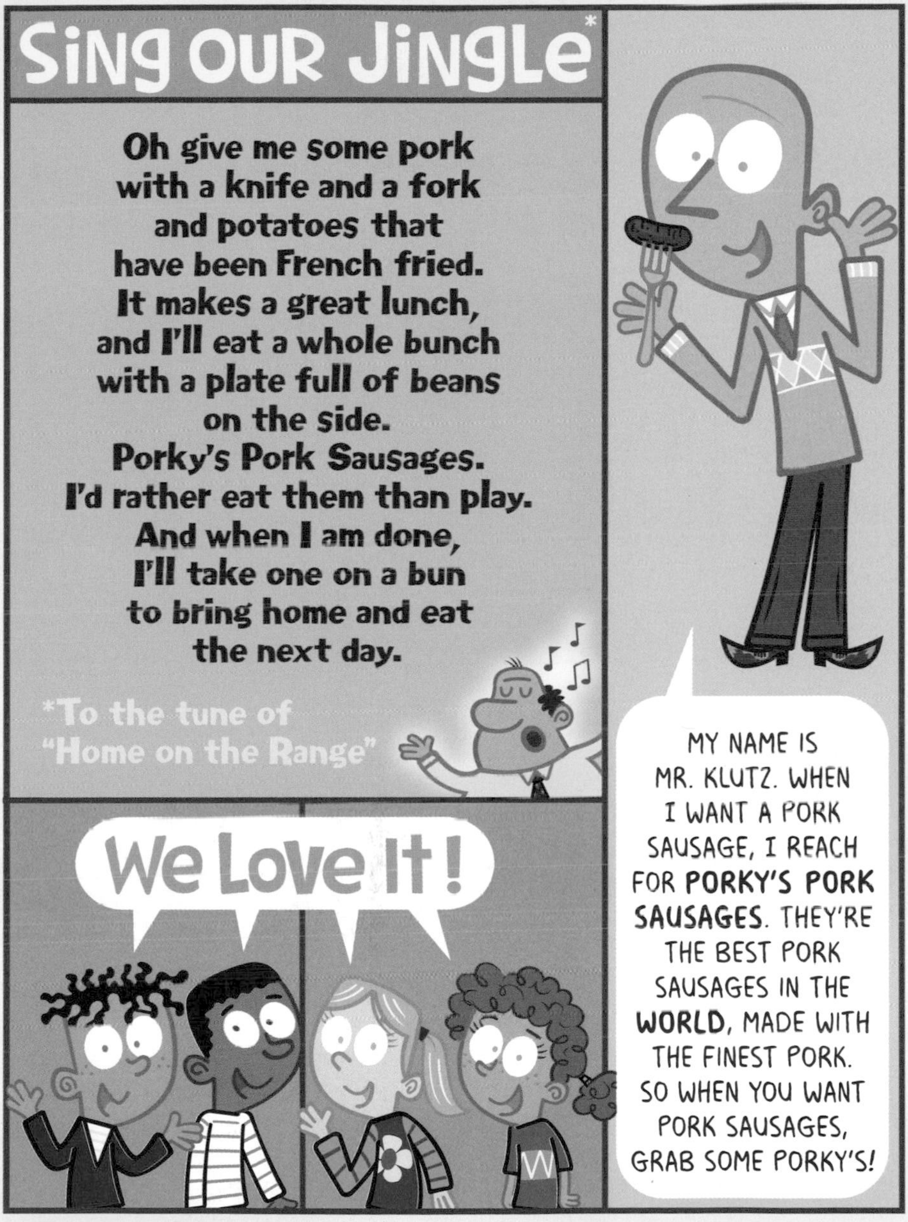
Sing Our Jingle*
Oh give me some pork
with a knife and a fork
and potatoes that
have been French fried.
It makes a great lunch,
and I'll eat a whole bunch
with a plate full of beans
on the side.
Porky's Pork Sausages.
I'd rather eat them than play.
And when I am done,
I'll take one on a bun
to bring home and eat
the next day.
*To the tune of
"Home on the Range"
MY NAME IS MR. KLUTZ. WHEN I WANT A PORK SAUSAGE, I REACH FOR PORKY'S PORK SAUSAGES. THEY'RE THE BEST PORK SAUSAGES IN THE WORLD, MADE WITH THE FINEST PORK. SO WHEN YOU WANT PORK SAUSAGES, GRAB SOME PORKY'S!
We Love It!

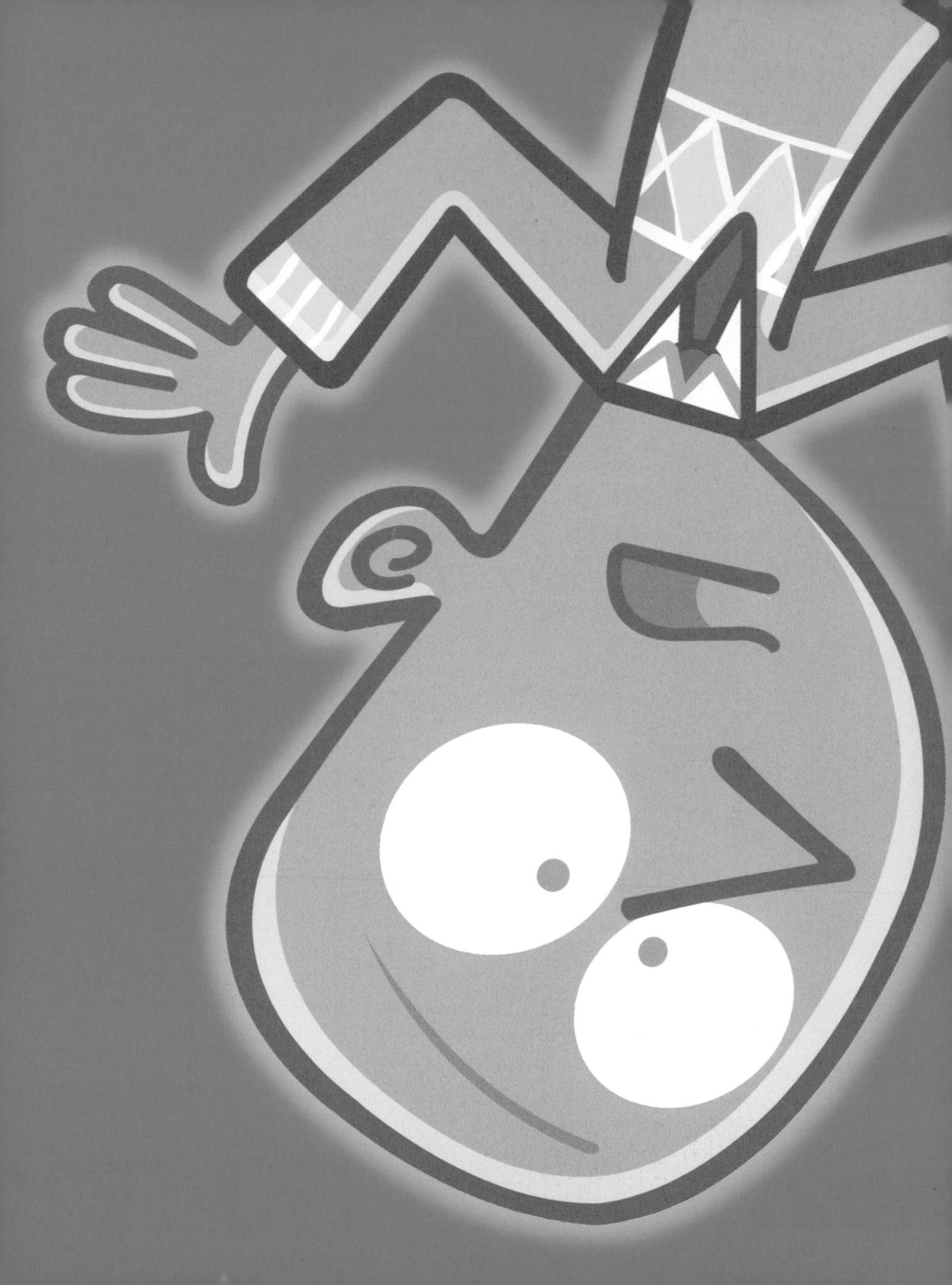

CHAPTER 5

Too Much Stuff

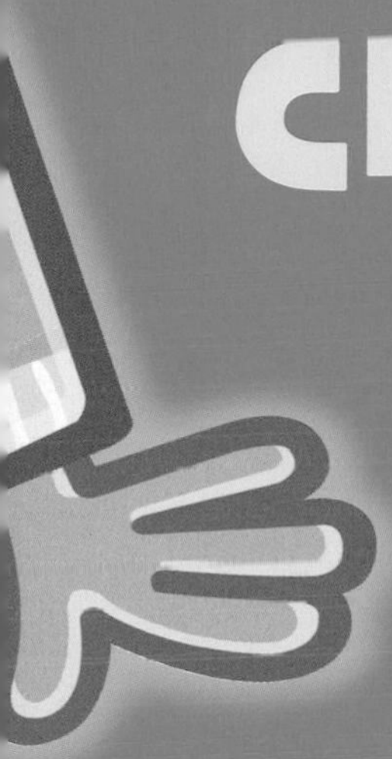

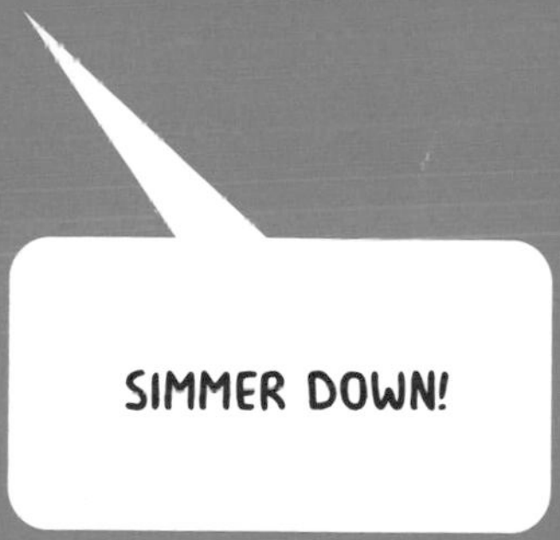
SIMMER DOWN!

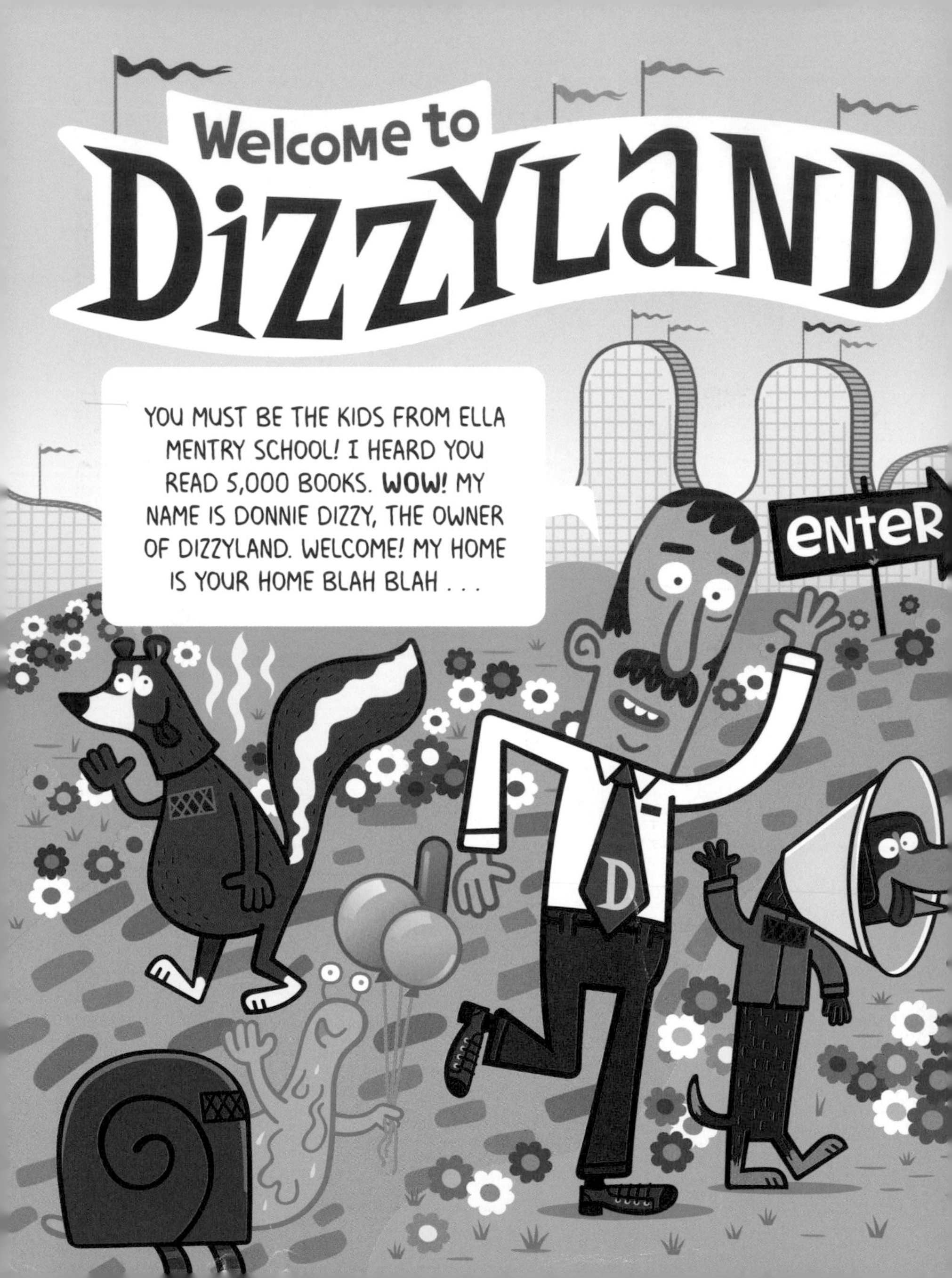

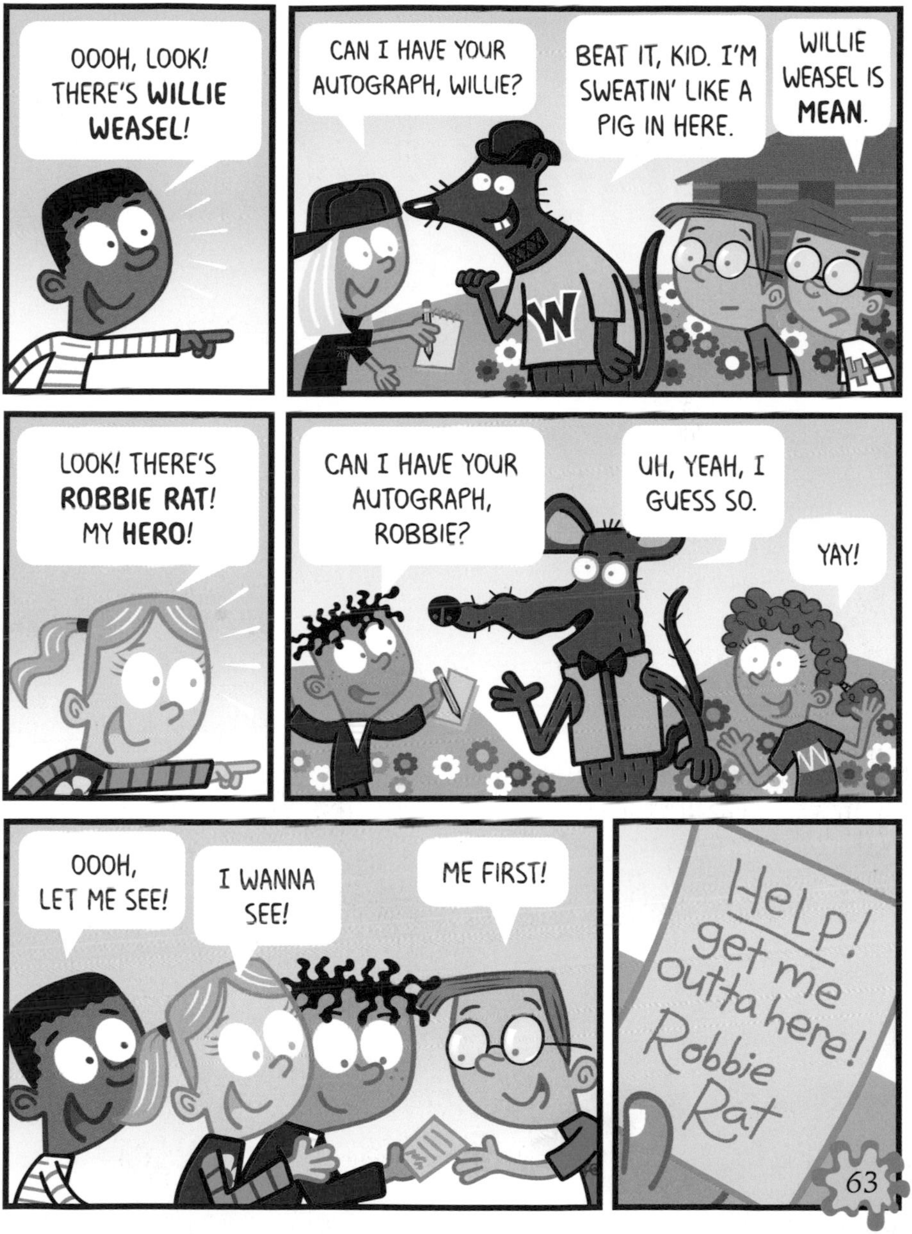
OOOH, LOOK! THERE'S WILLIE WEASEL!
CAN I HAVE YOUR AUTOGRAPH, WILLIE?
BEAT IT, KID. I'M SWEATIN' LIKE A PIG IN HERE.
WILLIE WEASEL IS MEAN.
LOOK! THERE'S ROBBIE RAT! MY HERO!
CAN I HAVE YOUR AUTOGRAPH, ROBBIE?
UH, YEAH, I GUESS SO.
YAY!
OOOH, LET ME SEE!
I WANNA SEE!
ME FIRST!
HeLP! get me outta here! Robbie Rat

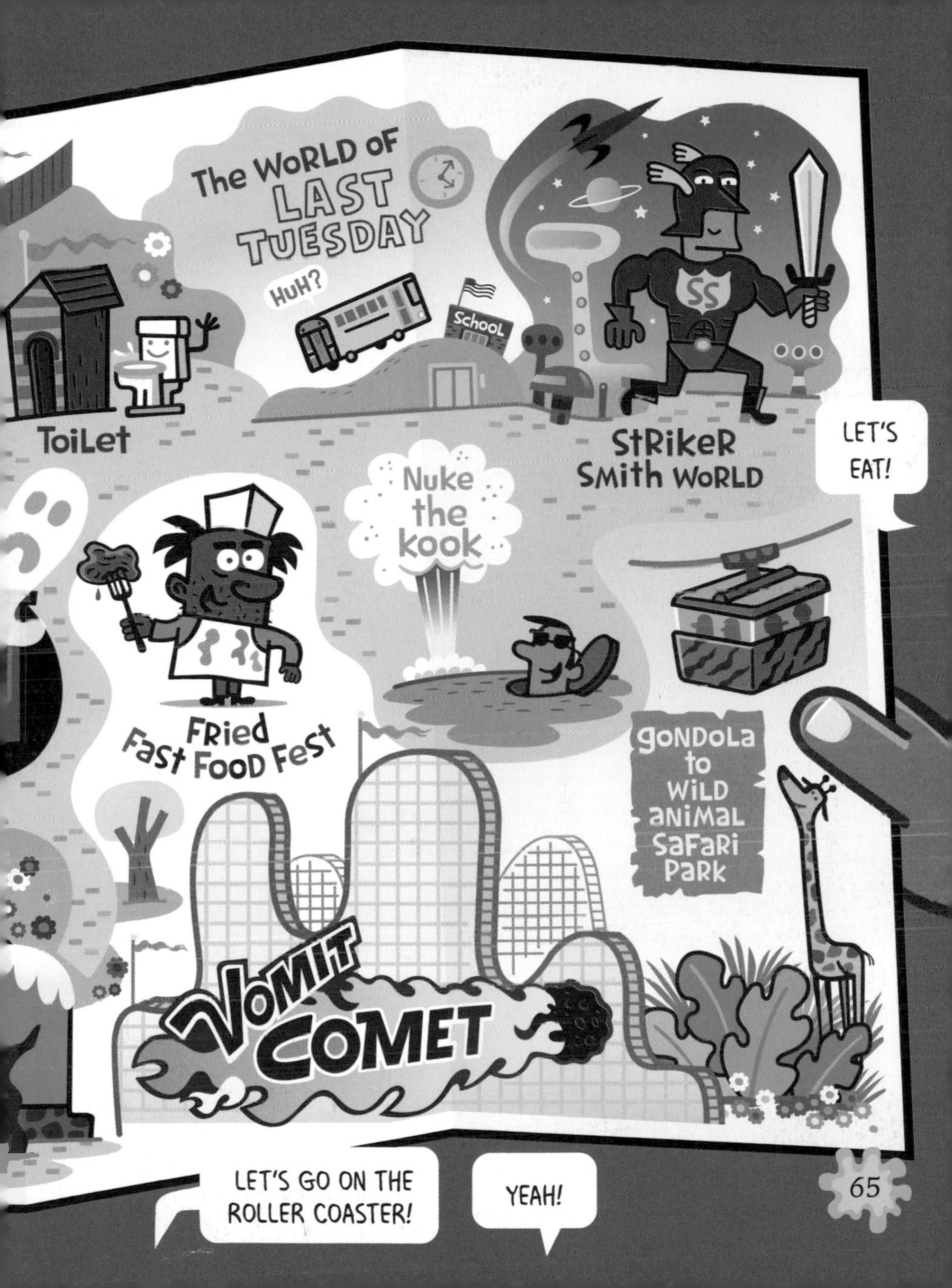
The WoRLD OF LAST TUESDAY
HUH?
School
ToiLet
StRikeR SMith WoRLD
LET'S EAT!
Nuke the kook
FRied Fast Food Fest
goNDoLa to WiLD aNiMaL SaFaRi PaRk
VoMIT COMET
LET'S GO ON THE ROLLER COASTER!
YEAH!

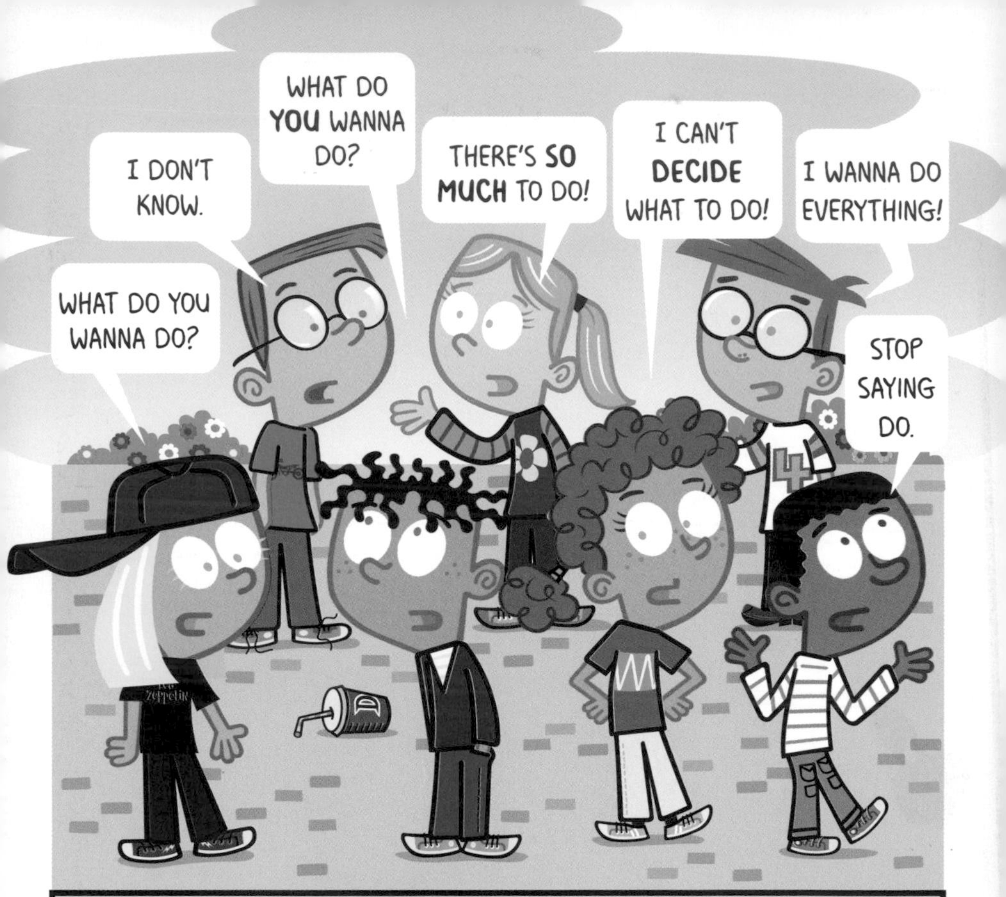
WHAT DO YOU WANNA DO?
I DON'T KNOW.
WHAT DO **YOU** WANNA DO?
THERE'S **SO MUCH** TO DO!
I CAN'T **DECIDE** WHAT TO DO!
I WANNA DO EVERYTHING!
STOP SAYING DO.

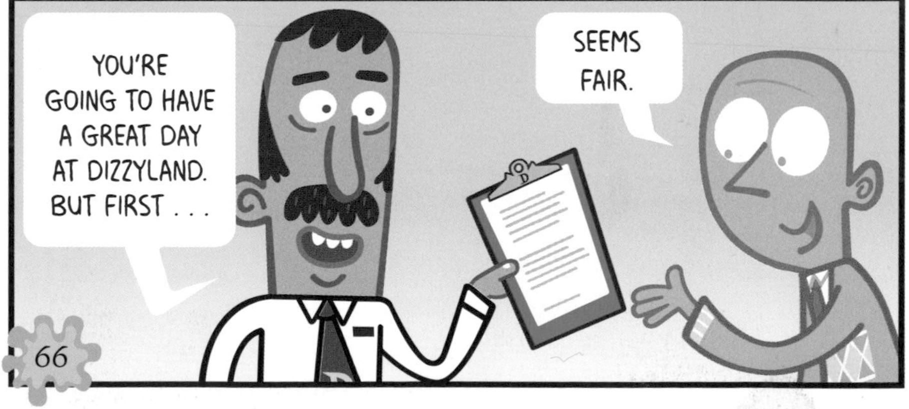
YOU'RE GOING TO HAVE A GREAT DAY AT DIZZYLAND. BUT FIRST . . .
SEEMS FAIR.

YOU CAN'T SUE US IF:

-Your personal items are lost or stolen.

-Your car is not in the parking lot at the end of the day.

-There is an earthquake, tornado, or natural disaster.

-One of the rides malfunctions.

-You get heat stroke while waiting on line.

-One of our toilets overflows while you're sitting on it.

-You don't have a good time.

-You're bored.

-You die.

-One of your parents is a lawyer.

-We put you in one of our promotional videos.

-We decide you're too ugly to appear in our promotional videos.

-You spend all your money on dumb souvenirs.

-One of our employees farts within five feet of you.

-You choke on your own vomit.

-You choke on somebody else's vomit.

-A mime follows you around, imitating you.

-An anvil falls on your head.

-You're hit by a boomerang.

-You slip on a banana peel.

-A banana peel slips on you.

-You don't like reading long lists of stuff.

-You fall into a sinkhole that suddenly opens up for no reason

-You get hit by a meteorite from outer space.

-Aliens from the future come and steal your car keys.

-You go blind after staring at a solar eclipse.

-One of the members of your party spontaneously combusts.

-You're trampled by a stampeding herd of buffalo.

-An atomic bomb wipes out the park while you're here.

-You get hit by a tranquilizing dart.

-Your intestines explode after you eat at our snack bar.

-Your body is dismembered by hungry wild animals.

-You get a paper cut signing this waiver.

Mr. Klutz

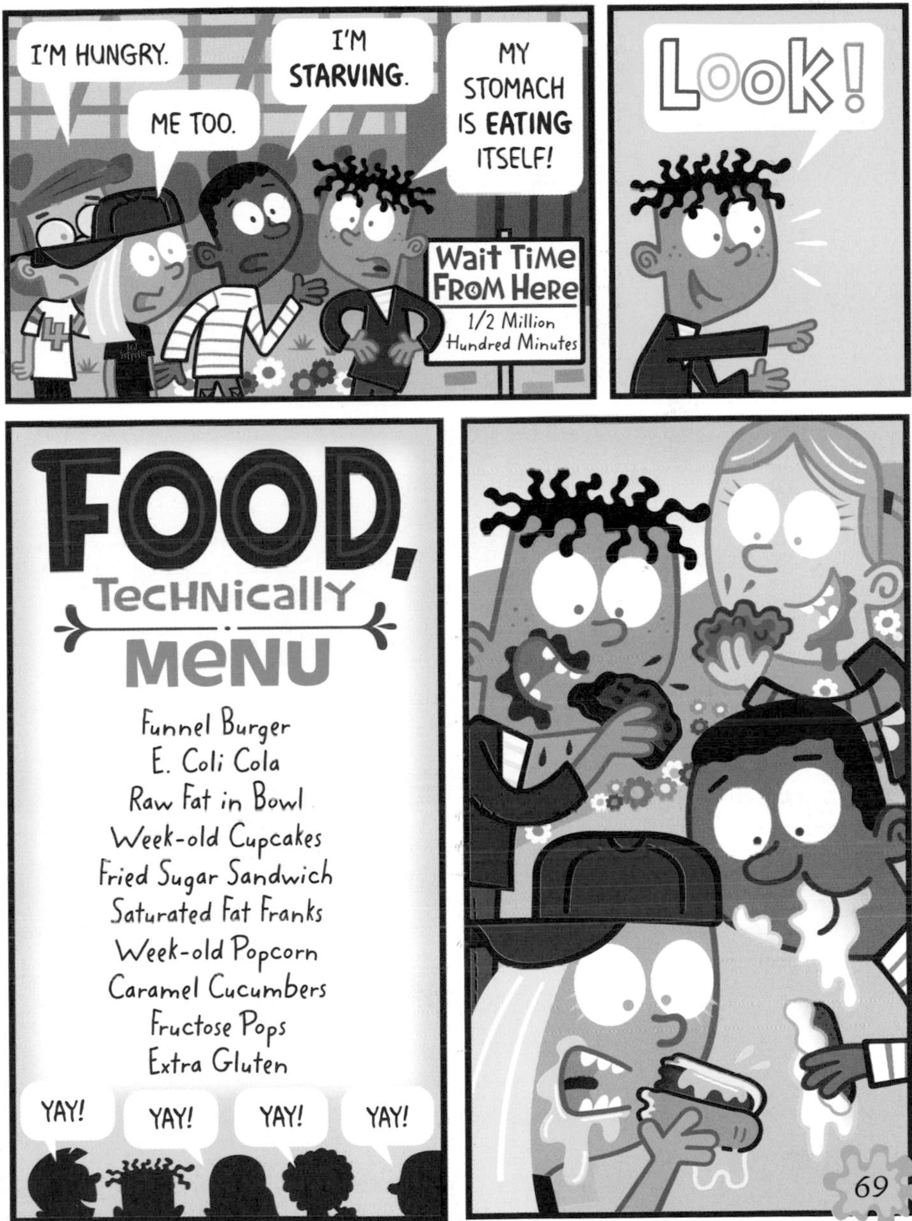
I'M HUNGRY.
ME TOO.
I'M STARVING.
MY STOMACH IS EATING ITSELF!
Wait Time From Here
1/2 Million Hundred Minutes
LOOK!
FOOD, TECHNICALLY MENU
Funnel Burger
E. Coli Cola
Raw Fat in Bowl
Week-old Cupcakes
Fried Sugar Sandwich
Saturated Fat Franks
Week-old Popcorn
Caramel Cucumbers
Fructose Pops
Extra Gluten
YAY!
YAY!
YAY!
YAY!

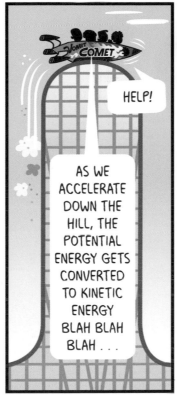

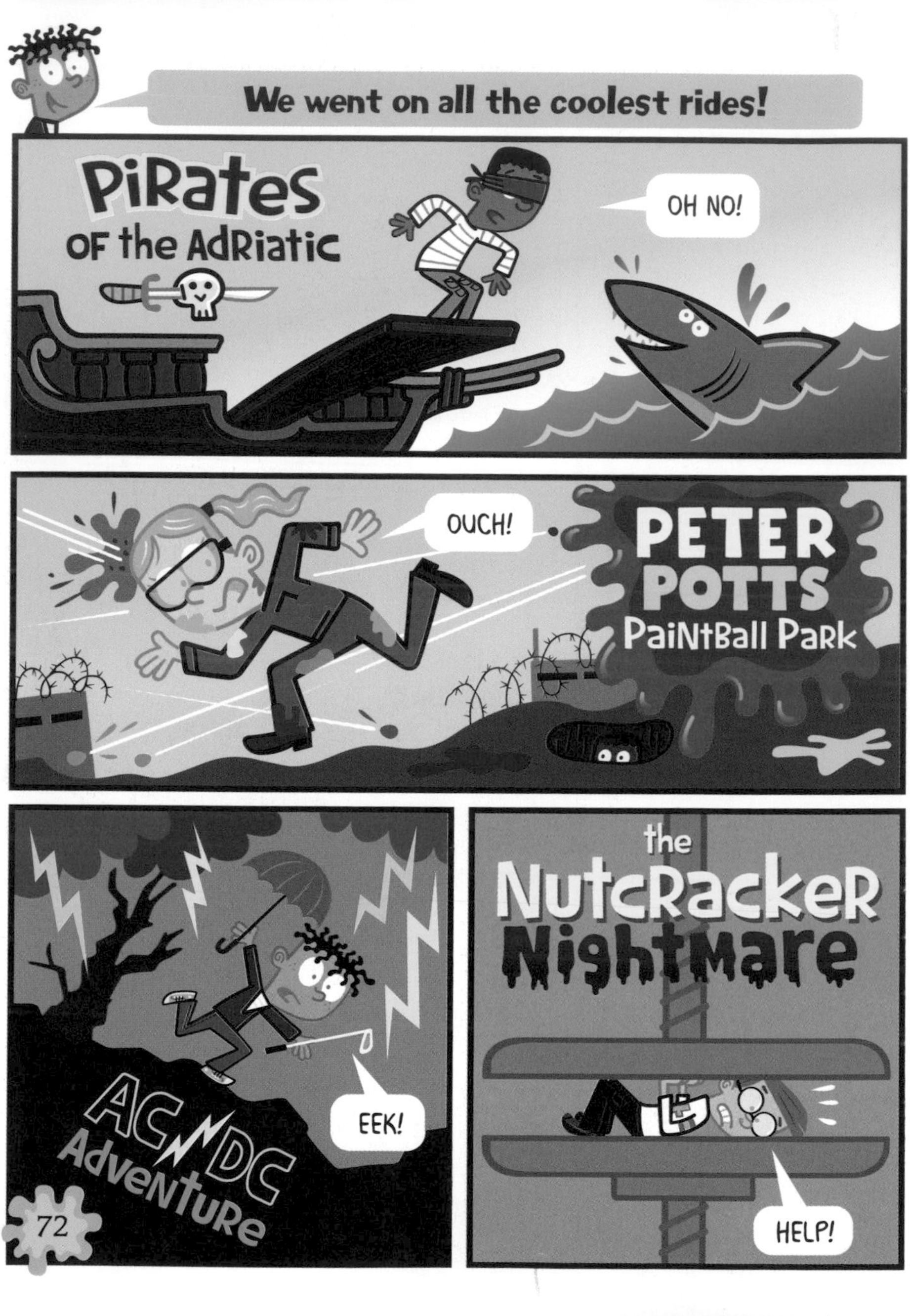
We went on all the coolest rides!
Pirates of the Adriatic
OH NO!
OUCH!
PETER POTTS PaintBall Park
AC/DC Adventure
EEK!
the NutcRacker Nightmare
HELP!

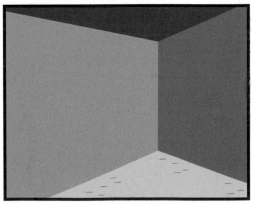

79

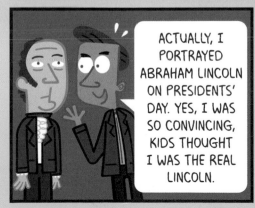

DO YOU KIDS WANT A SNEAK PEEK AT OUR NEWEST DIZZYLAND ATTRACTION?

YEAH!

SURE!

YOU BET!

HARVEY POTTER WORLD

I CALL IT . . .

HUH?*

(*Also **HUH** spelled backward.)

YES, IT'S ALL ABOUT A YOUNG WIZARD. HE GOES TO A SCHOOL CALLED LOGSMARTS . . .

UM . . .

82

HE CASTS SPELLS WITH THIS MAGIC WAND, WHICH YOU CAN BUY IN OUR GIFT SHOP . . .

Sale

UH, EXCUSE ME, MR. DIZZY . . .

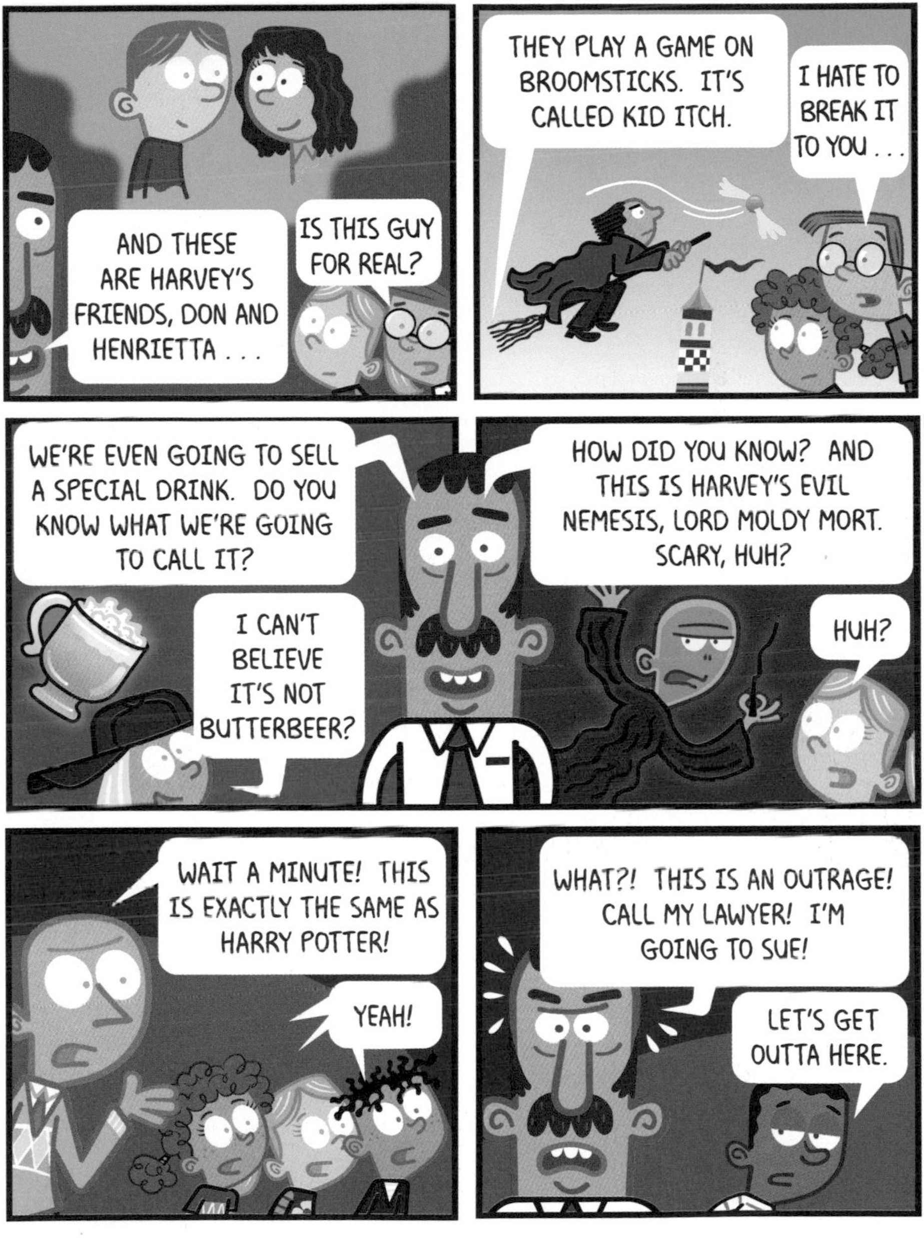
AND THESE ARE HARVEY'S FRIENDS, DON AND HENRIETTA . . .
IS THIS GUY FOR REAL?
THEY PLAY A GAME ON BROOMSTICKS. IT'S CALLED KID ITCH.
I HATE TO BREAK IT TO YOU . . .
WE'RE EVEN GOING TO SELL A SPECIAL DRINK. DO YOU KNOW WHAT WE'RE GOING TO CALL IT?
I CAN'T BELIEVE IT'S NOT BUTTERBEER?
HOW DID YOU KNOW? AND THIS IS HARVEY'S EVIL NEMESIS, LORD MOLDY MORT. SCARY, HUH?
HUH?
WAIT A MINUTE! THIS IS EXACTLY THE SAME AS HARRY POTTER!
YEAH!
WHAT?! THIS IS AN OUTRAGE! CALL MY LAWYER! I'M GOING TO SUE!
LET'S GET OUTTA HERE.

84

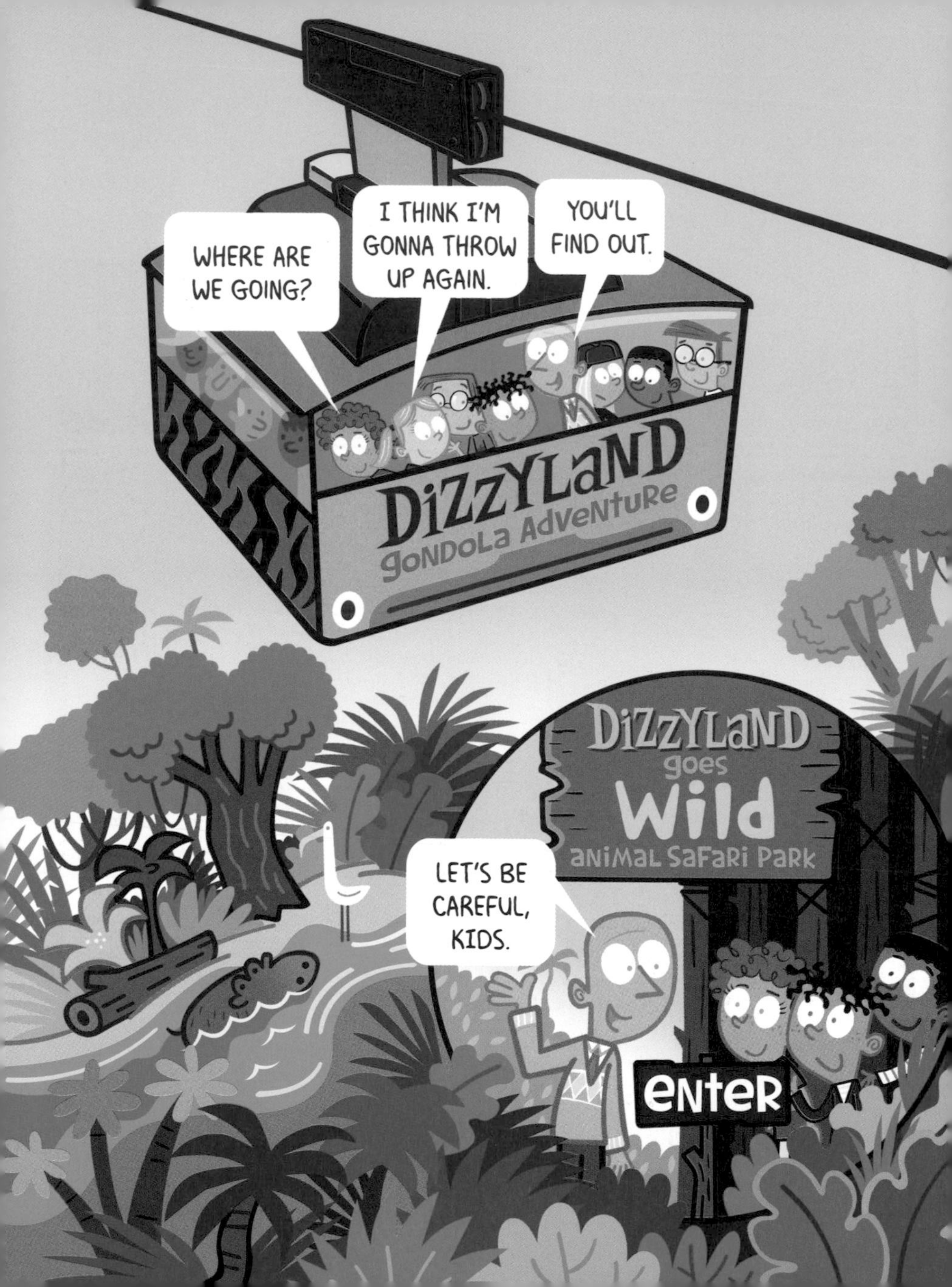
WHERE ARE WE GOING?
I THINK I'M GONNA THROW UP AGAIN.
YOU'LL FIND OUT.
DiZZYLaND
gONDoLa AdveNtuRe
DiZZYLaND goes Wild
aNiMaL SaFaRi PaRk
LET'S BE CAREFUL, KIDS.
eNTER

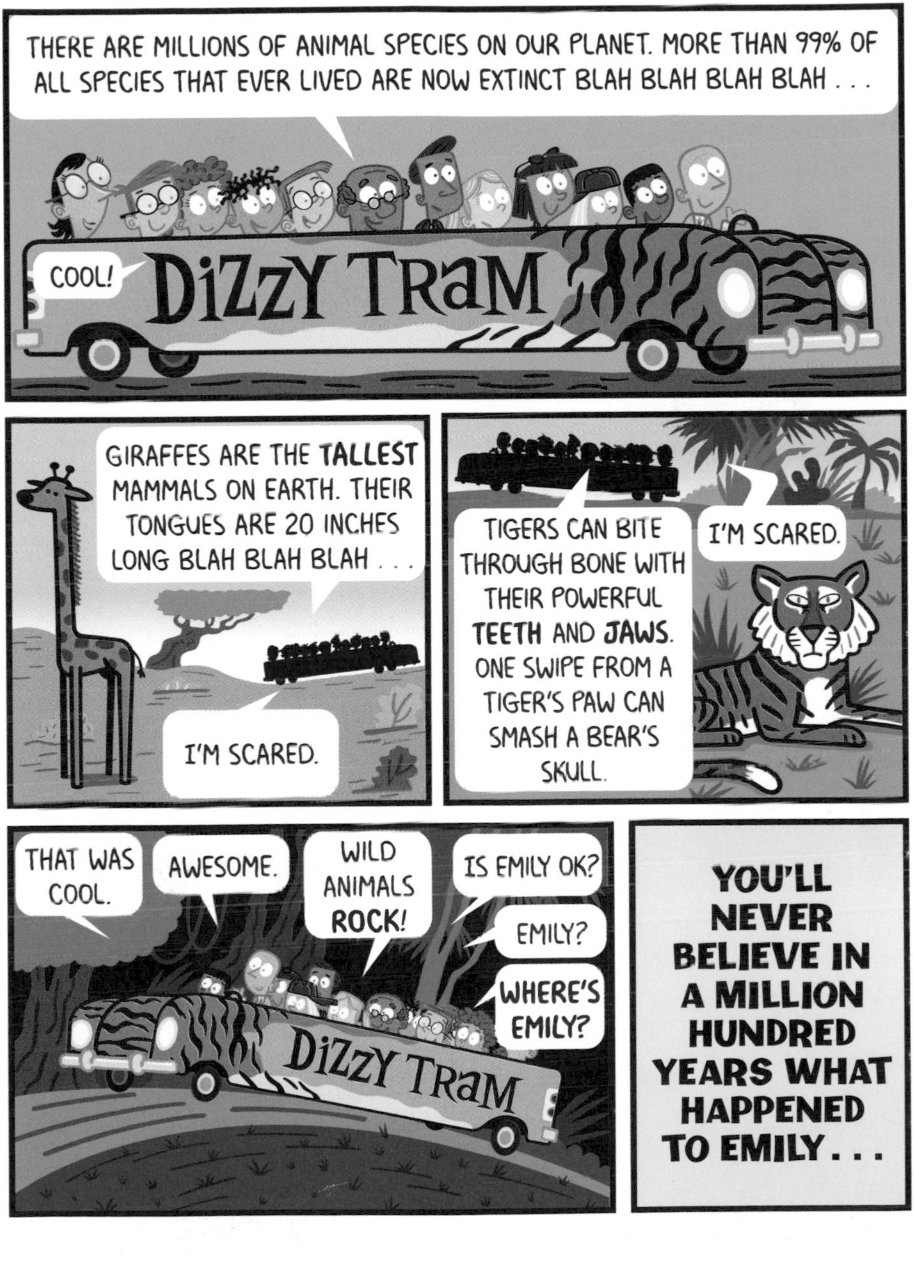
THERE ARE MILLIONS OF ANIMAL SPECIES ON OUR PLANET. MORE THAN 99% OF ALL SPECIES THAT EVER LIVED ARE NOW EXTINCT BLAH BLAH BLAH BLAH . . .
COOL!
DiZzY TRaM
GIRAFFES ARE THE **TALLEST** MAMMALS ON EARTH. THEIR TONGUES ARE 20 INCHES LONG BLAH BLAH BLAH . . .
I'M SCARED.
TIGERS CAN BITE THROUGH BONE WITH THEIR POWERFUL **TEETH** AND **JAWS**. ONE SWIPE FROM A TIGER'S PAW CAN SMASH A BEAR'S SKULL.
I'M SCARED.
THAT WAS COOL.
AWESOME.
WILD ANIMALS **ROCK!**
IS EMILY OK?
EMILY?
WHERE'S EMILY?
DiZzY TRaM
YOU'LL NEVER BELIEVE IN A MILLION HUNDRED YEARS WHAT HAPPENED TO EMILY . . .

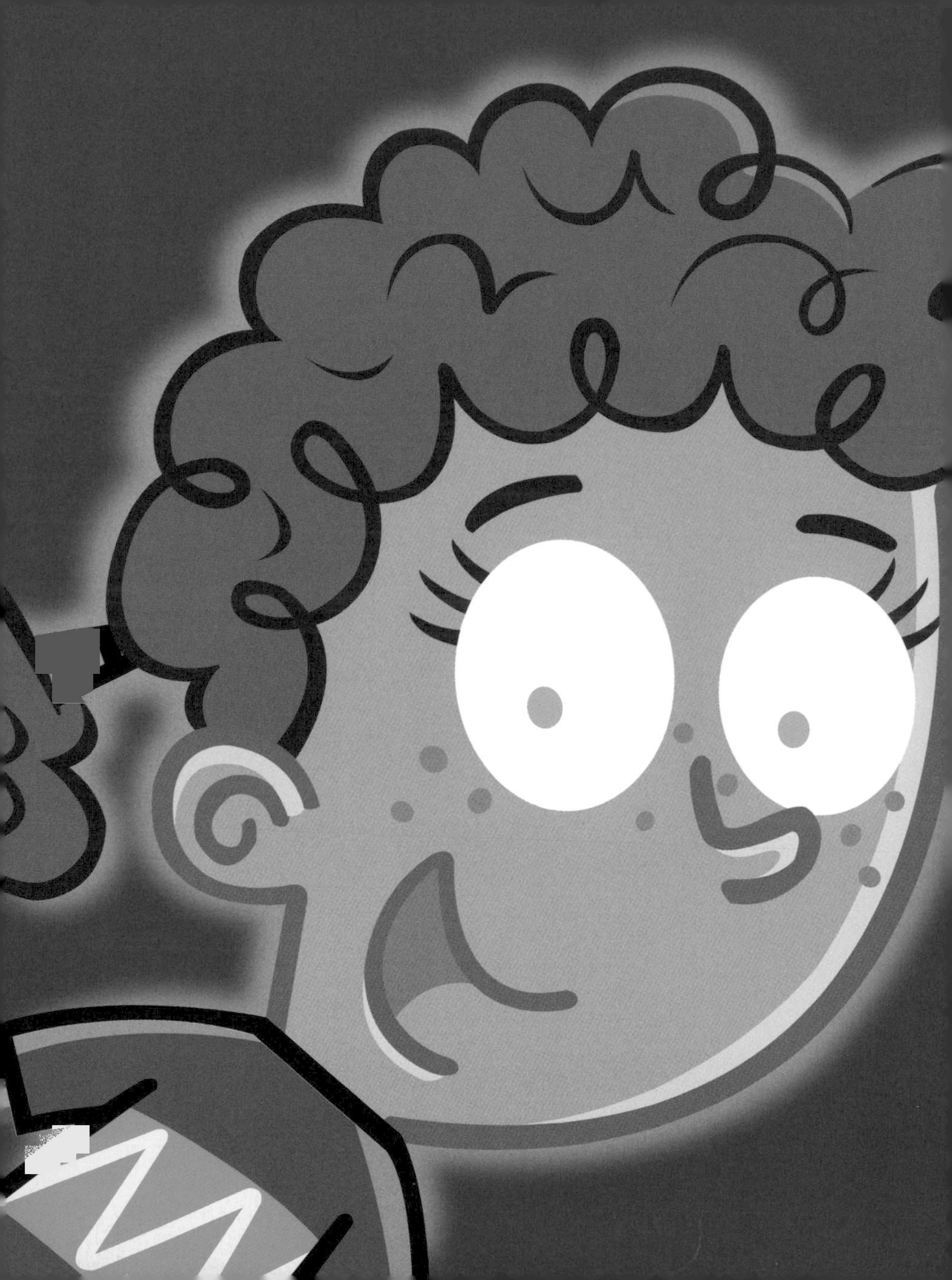

CHAPteR 6

We Should Really Get Rid of Some of This Stuff!

I LOVE
SURPRISE
ENDINGS!

92

93

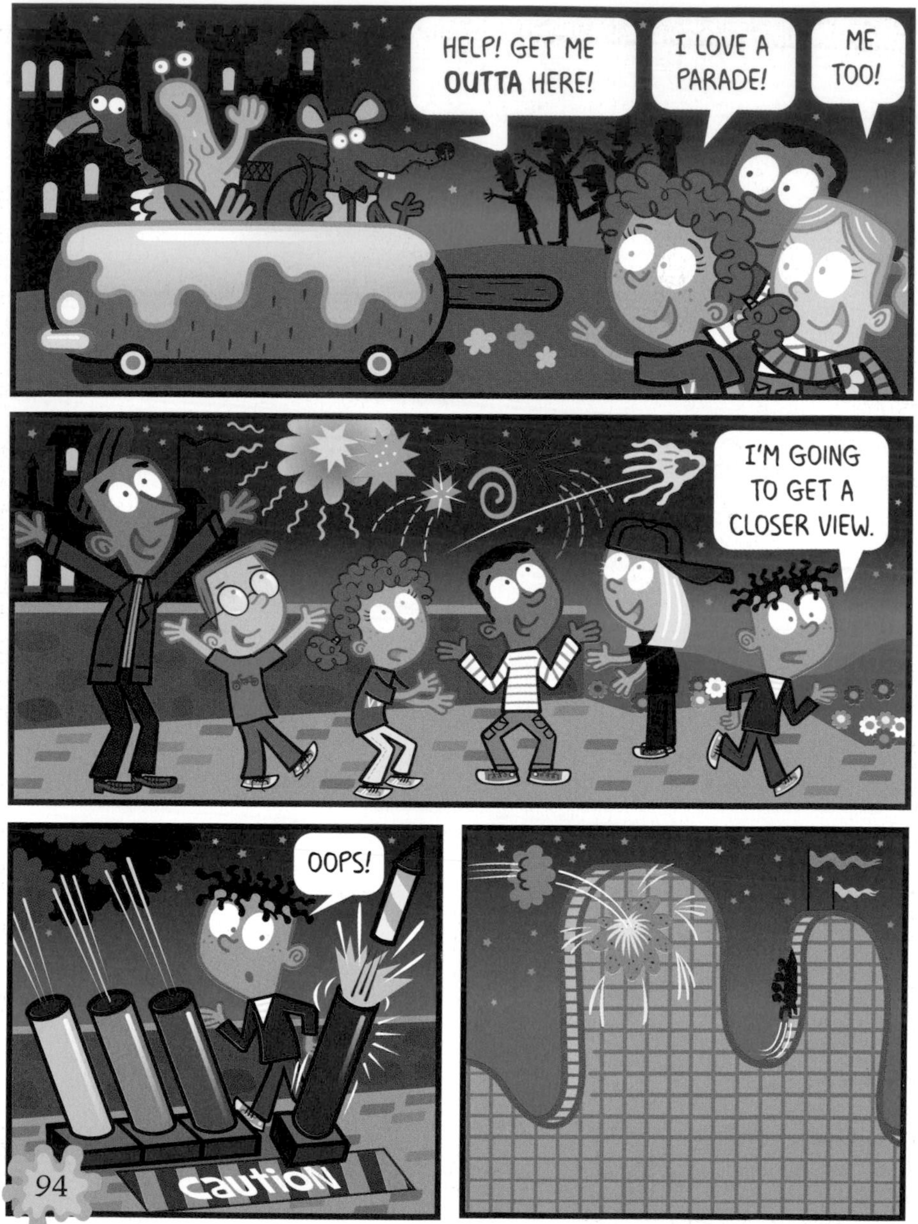
HELP! GET ME **OUTTA** HERE!
I LOVE A PARADE!
ME TOO!
I'M GOING TO GET A CLOSER VIEW.
OOPS!
CAUTION

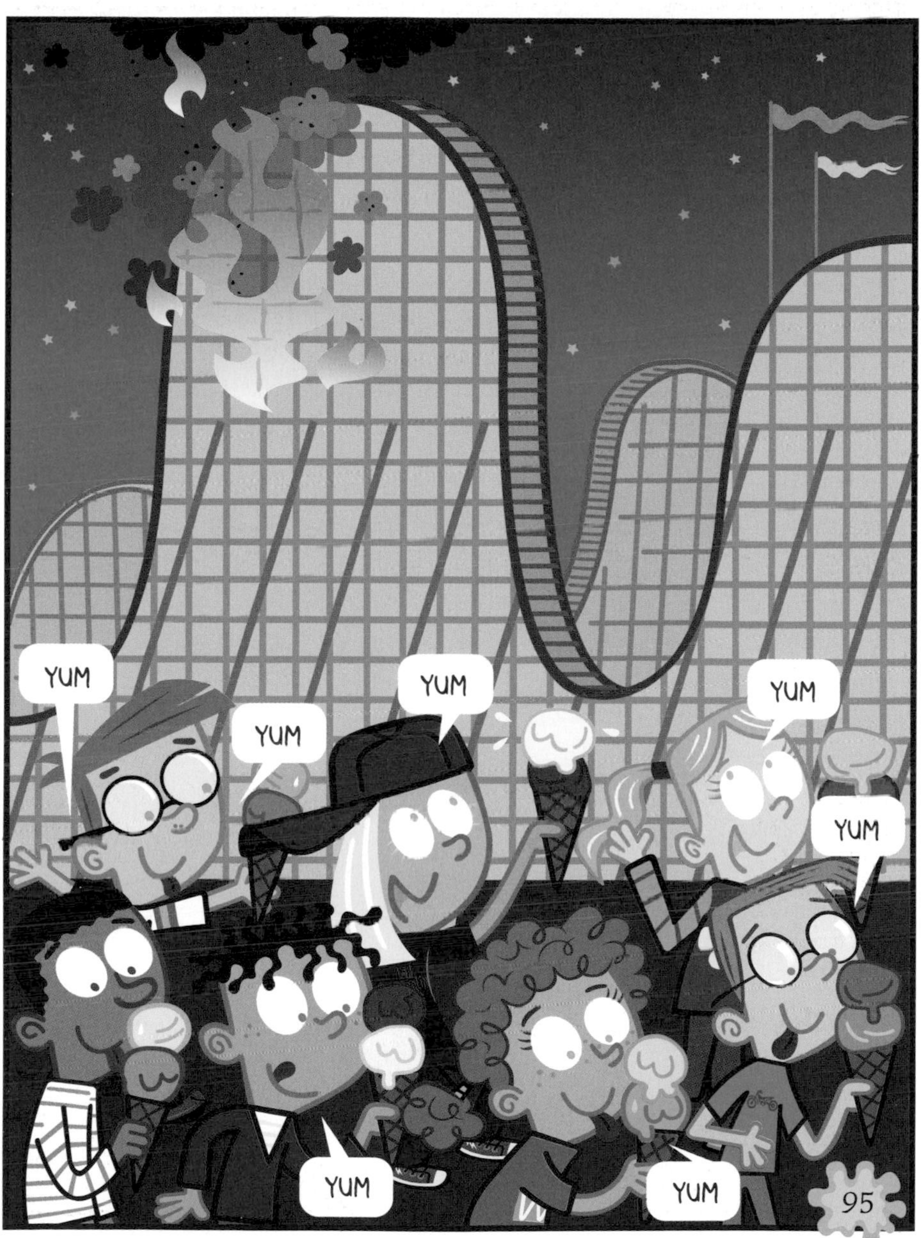
YUM
YUM
YUM
YUM
YUM
YUM
YUM

96

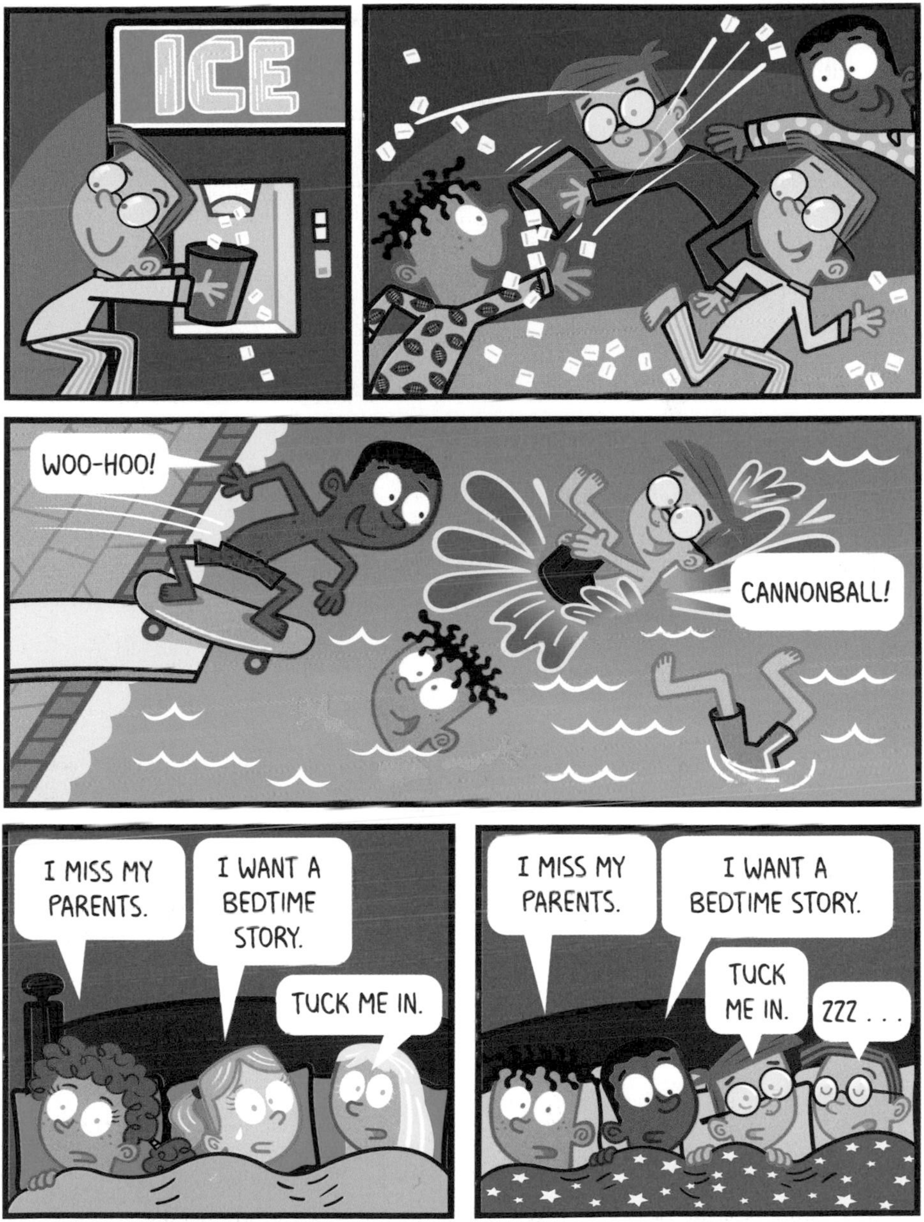
ICE
WOO-HOO!
CANNONBALL!
I MISS MY PARENTS.
I WANT A BEDTIME STORY.
TUCK ME IN.
I MISS MY PARENTS.
I WANT A BEDTIME STORY.
TUCK ME IN.
ZZZ . . .

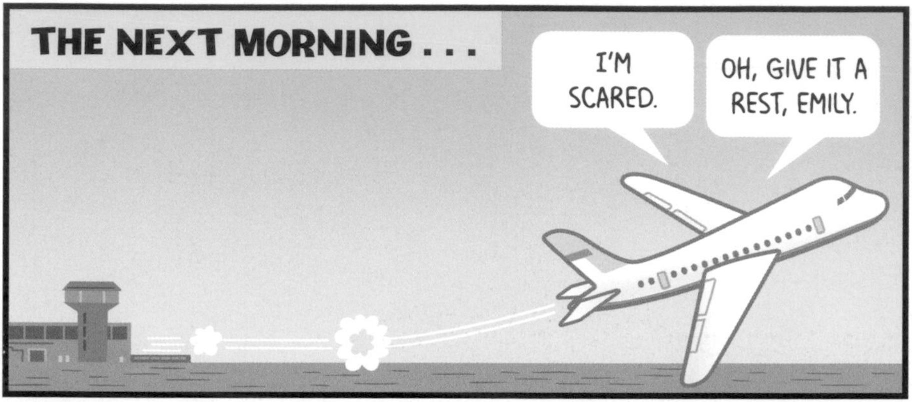
THE NEXT MORNING . . .
I'M SCARED.
OH, GIVE IT A REST, EMILY.

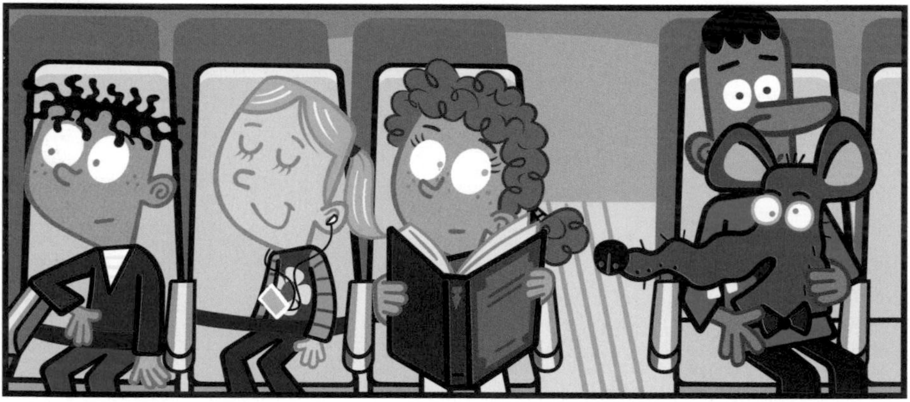

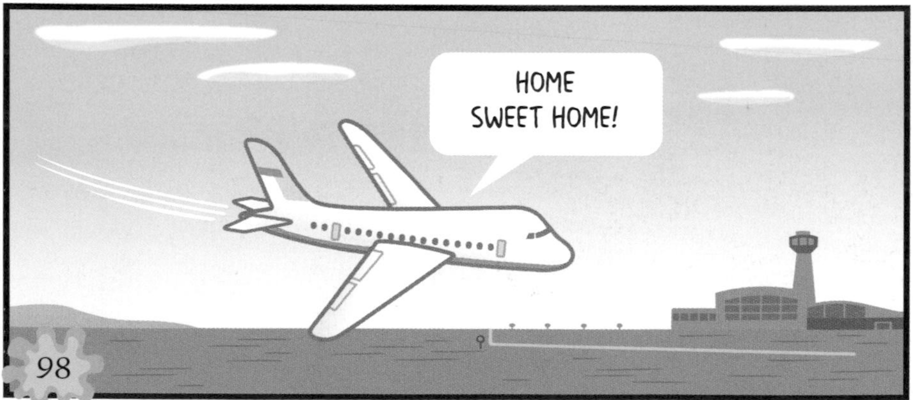
HOME SWEET HOME!

MEANWHILE, BACK AT ELLÁ MENTRY SCHOOL . . .

ON ONE ACRE OF LAND, THERE CAN BE A MILLION EARTHWORMS. THEY CAN EAT THEIR WEIGHT EACH DAY. WORMS BREATHE THROUGH THEIR SKIN.

THERE ARE MILLIONS OF ANIMAL SPECIES ON OUR PLANET. MORE THAN 99% OF ALL SPECIES THAT EVER LIVED ARE NOW EXTINCT.

PHYSICS IS THE STUDY OF HOW THINGS MOVE.

GIRAFFES ARE THE **TALLEST** MAMMALS ON EARTH. THEIR TONGUES ARE 20 INCHES LONG.

MOTION SICKNESS IS CAUSED WHEN YOUR EYES AND THE BALANCE CENTERS IN YOUR EARS DISAGREE. FOOD THAT COMES BACK UP IS SQUEEZED FROM YOUR INTESTINES INTO YOUR STOMACH AND THEN UP YOUR THROAT.

AS A ROLLER COASTER ACCELERATES DOWN A HILL, THE POTENTIAL ENERGY GETS CONVERTED TO KINETIC ENERGY. THE ENERGY CHANGES FROM STORED ENERGY TO MOVING ENERGY.

WHEN A PLANE MOVES FORWARD, THE CURVED WINGS CUT THE AIRFLOW IN HALF. SOME AIR GOES ABOVE THE WING, AND SOME GOES BELOW IT. THE DIFFERENCE IN AIR PRESSURE GENERATES A FORCE CALLED LIFT.

YOU CAN'T DESTROY THIS SCHOOL! THESE KIDS ARE SMART. THEIR TEACHERS MUST BE **AMAZING!**

CARBLES TOXIC WASTE INC.

GRRR . . .

103

AND SO THE CONFLICT IS OVER . . . FOR NOW. THANKS TO THE BRAVE LEADERSHIP OF MR. KLUTZ AND HIS SMALL BAND OF REBEL EDUCATORS AND STUDENTS, PEACE AND ORDER HAVE BEEN RESTORED. THE GREEDY AND RUTHLESS DR. CARBLES HAS BEEN EXILED TO THE FARTHEST CORNERS OF THE SCHOOL SYSTEM. HIS OBSESSION WITH DESTROYING ELLA MENTRY SCHOOL MAY HAVE BEEN TEMPORARILY INTERRUPTED, BUT THE MERCILESS DR. CARBLES LIVES ON TO FIGHT ANOTHER DAY. WHO KNOWS WHEN HE MIGHT RISE FROM THE ASHES, MORE DESPERATE THAN EVER, AND RETURN TO INFLICT PAIN AND TYRANNY ON ALL THOSE WHO STAND IN HIS WAY? HOW LONG WILL THE FORCES OF GOOD- NESS AND NICENESS BE ABLE TO RESIST THIS RELENTLESS ONSLAUGHT OF EVIL?

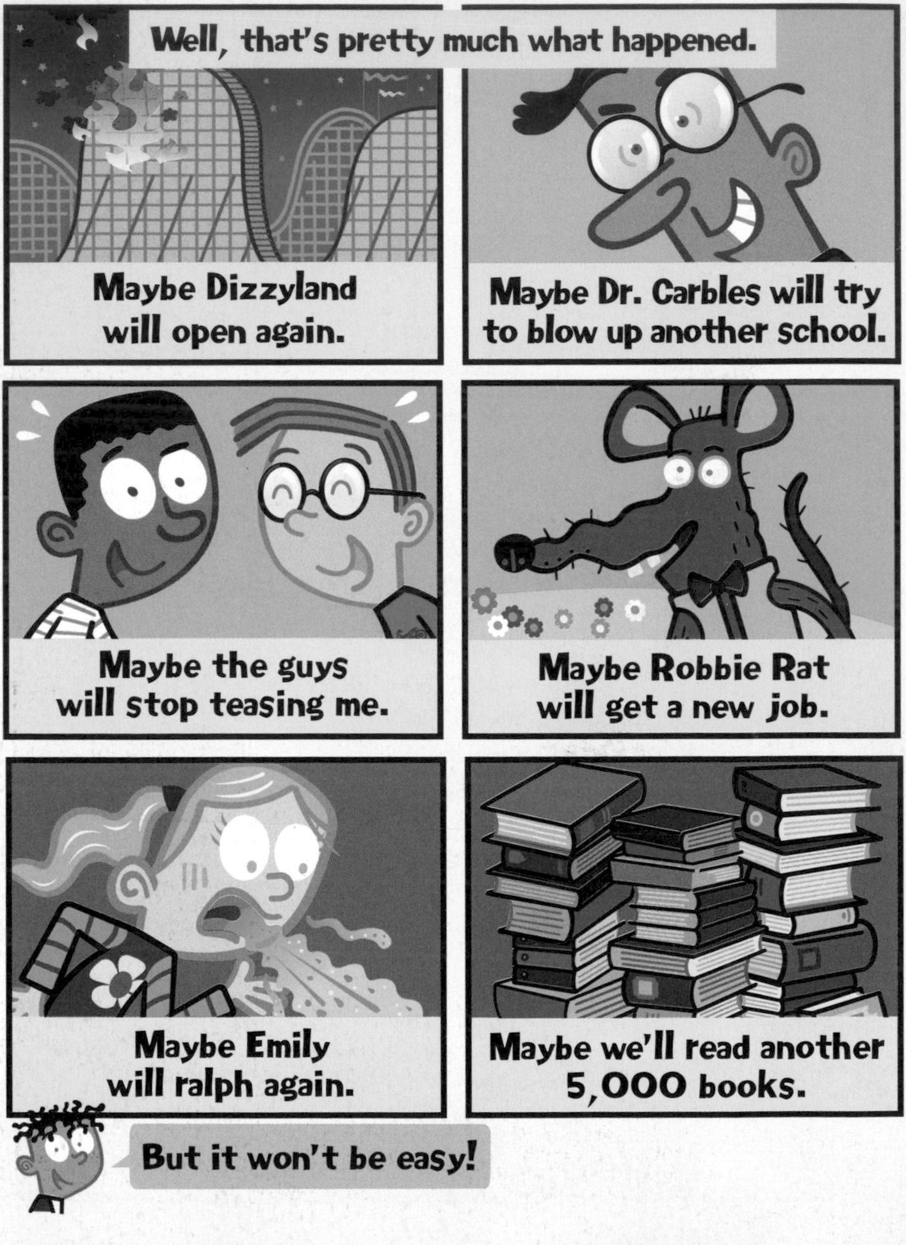
Well, that's pretty much what happened.
Maybe Dizzyland will open again.
Maybe Dr. Carbles will try to blow up another school.
Maybe the guys will stop teasing me.
Maybe Robbie Rat will get a new job.
Maybe Emily will ralph again.
Maybe we'll read another 5,000 books.
But it won't be easy!